CELESTIAL REQUESTS

Charles Stacey

ARTHUR H. STOCKWELL LTD
Torrs Park, Ilfracombe, Devon, EX34 8BA
Established 1898
www.ahstockwell.co.uk

British Library Cataloguing-in-Publication Data.
A catalogue record for this book is available
from the British Library.

This is a work of fiction. Names, characters, places and incidents are the product of the author's imagination and any resemblance to actual persons, living or dead, events or locales, is purely coincidental.

By the same author:
Beyond All Horizons

ISBN 978-0-7223-4566-5
Printed in Great Britain by
Arthur H. Stockwell Ltd
Torrs Park   Ilfracombe
Devon EX34 8BA

To three wonderful people; Caroline, Robin and Christopher.
And to all the charities working to help, aid and succour the distressed and suffering particularly the children worldwide.

INTRODUCTION

I wish I could say with truthfulness what Charles Dickens said in his preface to the 1860 edition of David Copperfield, namely 'Of all my books, I like this the best!' He went on to say (or 'pursued' a word he gave to continuity in conversational terms), 'It will easily be believed that I am a fond parent to every child of my fancy, and that no one can ever love that family as dearly as I love them. But, like many fond parents, I have in my heart of hearts a favourite child, and his name is David Copperfield.'

As this is only the second published book I have written I cannot emulate in full the introduction made by Charles Dickens. I can, however, say that Conan Derrick Holmes, perspicacious lover of Peace Poetry and Pleasantries of Speech, is a favourite character of my fanciful imagination. A former Chief Investigating Officer in Headquarters Nimbus 9, and, as a result of his onerous workload in the former book *Beyond all Horizons*, he had a serious heart attack. A long-term convalescence was advised, all medical advice diligently followed, and is well enough to take up a different calling. For a long time he had considered that the 'Celestial Request Archives' at HQ Nimbus 9, contained a wealth of detail relating to the good works undertaken by H.C. – the person to whom, in the form of a Special Friend – they had been directed. The stories in this book are, in the main, his work, assisted by his carer/secretary, Nurse Constance Lamal Dickens. Both H.C. (Highest Celeste, the Wise, Humane, Senior Authority, on Nimbus 9) and his new private secretary, Charles Easton, were quite taken by the literary skills of Holmes and put together a short story or two of their own. If there is an inordinate stress on Happy Endings to many of the stories Holmes accepts full responsibility. As he once said to Charles Easton, 'There is no custodial sentence for wearing your heart on your sleeve.' All at Nimbus 9 are grateful for the fact he has two sleeves for that magnanimous heart of his for display purposes.

CONTENTS

CHAPTER 1

OCEANIA

'Do you know, Easton,' said H.C. to his companion as they sat in the fresh morning sunshine on easy chairs on the balcony at HQ Nimbus 9, 'that I rather like the way Holmes always manages to develop a happy ending to those stories he writes on some of the Celestial Requests we receive.'

'Yes, he does have a way with words. His reports to me, when he was my Chief Investigating Officer, always seemed to have a few lines of poetry or 'Sumptuous Prose' as he styled it in them. Made them human, he said.'

He and that charming secretary, Connie Dickens are at the moment attending on my behalf the homecoming of our rescue schooner *Oceania* from its recent voyages. He and Connie wanted to attend in order to accept into their care, a small four-year-old boy, who when playing with other youngsters, lost his footing on a jetty and fell into the sea and was carried away by strong currents and drowned. His parents tried desperately to save him, but without success. I had a Request to take care of the little boy who was described as loveable and lively and so greatly loved by all who knew him. I could not think of a better guardian for the little lad's acceptance than that warm-hearted Derrick Holmes, and of course, Constance

Dickens will be there to provide that comforting touch for the little soul. All those we save over the years, as you well know, Easton, are a little bewildered at first on their homecoming. They all wish first of all to send their messages of safe arrival to those they love and miss so much – and, it is a busy time for us processing those desperate notifications out. This was the case, as you know, Easton, when there had been a great loss of lives at sea.

I remember vividly the anguish caused one January many years ago when the *Willhelm Gustaff* was sunk by a submarine in the Baltic Sea occasioning the loss of over 9,000 people, and of course, many other great losses of life throughout that cruel inhuman conflict waging worldwide between the years 1939 and 1945. Our rescue vessel was constantly used. Nature's blows are hard enough to bear at sea, without the need to resort to armoured warfare on the high seas. But it is my long-held hope to see saner policies prevail in that world Holmes refers to as a personal Speck of Dust.

'I've always liked Holmes. I can visualise him sitting at the boy's side helping him with his little note to his parents and the rest of the family. You are good at descriptive narrative, Easton, how might it have taken place?'

'I don't usually make a good fist of assumptive prose, H.C., but it might just have gone a little like this:

'I believe that when the little lad asked Holmes for his help in writing his letter, it was because he did not do "joined-up" writing very well, but was going to be very good at it when he went to school like his sisters, and he asked Holmes if he was a school teacher.'

'No,' replied Holmes.

'Well I like you helping me like one. But what do you do at school?'

'I'm a kind of detective,' Holmes replied.

'Do you detect people?'

'Yes, but in a nice way.'

'Why do you detect them, if they are nice people?'

'Because we need nice people to become Guardian Angels.'

'What do Guardian Angels do then?'

'They take care of people and see they come to no harm. And try to make them happy and to help others. It goes round in a nice big happy kind of circle. You know what a circle is, don't you?'

'Oh yes! My old football is a circle and my school cap when I get one, will have a circle in it for my head top – could I be one of those angels?'

'Well, yes, but as you are young, you would be looking after children first – then later, when you can write joined-up letters, you could guide grown-ups like your mother and father.'

'And my sisters?'

'Yes, of course.'

'And all my big family?'

'Yes, lots and lots of people and boys and girls need help too.'

'And we have a kitten called Kitty Kat so I could help her too?'

'Yes, but we must try to write your special letter now. How would you like it to start?'

'Well, you say something nice to my mummy and daddy first and tell them I love them and miss them and my sisters and Kitty Kat (don't forget her milk!), and tell them that I have you as my best friend here and you are going to teach me to be a Guardian Angel.'

'I believe Holmes was quite touched by the little lad's expression of affection for him, that should the letter bear any smudge, blot or blurring, one can but assume Holmes inadvertently added a lachrymose touch of his own.'

'Yes, but knowing Holmes, he'd say they were commas, or simply marks of his punctilious mind.'

'Would you believe it, Easton, if so apprised?'

'Yes, I think so, but with very slight misgivings of course.'

'Of course, Easton, of course.'

CHAPTER 2

BUTTERCUPS AND DAISIES

'Holmsey,' said the little boy to the former Chief Investigating Officer, Conan Derrick Holmes, his adopted friend at Nimbus 9. 'When you go on another detecting nice people trip, could I come with you?'

'Any special reason for that question, young man?' replied Holmes.

'Well, I could tell my mummy and daddy and my sister that you are taking care of me until they come here and stay with me always.'

'I would have to get special permission for you to come with me, as it is a long journey and we travel at a very fast speed – perhaps too fast for small boys.'

'But I shall be a lot bigger when I am five next week,' replied the boy confidently.

'Yes, of course, that does make a big difference,' replied Holmes approvingly. 'I shall see what can be arranged – but if it isn't approved, can I do anything special for you when I go on my travels?'

'Well,' said the boy, obviously disappointed at the qualifying remark, 'you could get one of the flowers my mummy likes and put it on her pillow. Then she will know I am safe and well. It will be quicker than a letter to them if you could do that for me, don't you think it is a good idea, if I can't go with you?'

'A very good idea,' said Holmes approvingly, 'and what flower shall it be?'

'A buttercup,' said the boy animatedly. 'I used to pick one for her from our garden and give it to her under her chin to see if she liked butter.'

'And did she?' said Holmes mischievously.

'Oh yes, and we all had some for our tea, as well.'

Holmes, in his wisdom, knew his next visit would probably be long after the buttercup had ceased to grow on the Speck of Dust but knew he could arrange such a horticultural floral season digression on behalf of his small, eager-faced charge.

'Yes,' he replied briskly, 'I can most certainly do that small errand for you. Any other message to be left there for you?'

'Oh no, Holmsey, Mummy will know it is from me. A big thank you, Holmsey, and I'll do my joined-up writing lessons with Aunt Connie when you are away – I promise.'

And both the boy and Holmes kept their respective promises.

On the morning of a cold December day, the boy's mother, on awakening found in midwinter, the buttercup left surreptitiously by Holmes during the night hours. It lay on the pillow beside her head, and as she stirred it fell beneath her face. She gently picked it up and knew instantly its sender. Tears not of sorrow, but of grateful relief welled for a moment on her lower eyelid before tumbling down her cheek. Her husband, who had risen earlier, entered with the morning cup of tea, and seeing her weeping and smiling at the same time, sat beside her on the edge of the bed. He saw her hands clutching, so lightly, the small green stem of the flower, and said, 'There you are, my love, we always knew he was safe and would let us know one day in some way or another. It was always our special secret, my dear, and it always will be until that special day. Well, I'm off to the office and will give you a call later.'

As he left the house, thinking deeply about the matter, he

nearly collided with a tall gentleman who apologised swiftly, 'My fault, old chap, sorry. I was thinking of other things.'

'How odd,' said the father, 'so too was I.'

'Great minds obviously think alike,' said Holmes as he went on his way, smiling.

'I suppose they do,' mused the father as he too went on his way, with a smile on his face, equally as large as that of Holmes.

After yet another successful mission, Holmes returned to Nimbus 9 to be congratulated by all appropriate authorities and to a rapturous welcome by the small boy sitting at his studies with Nurse Connie Dickens beside him.

Connie ran to embrace him but the young lad was swifter and leapt into the welcoming open arms awaiting him. 'Did she know it was from me?'

'But from who else, my bonny lad? She knew at once it was from you – and kissed it gently, like this.' He placed his lips on the lad's forehead and looked at Connie and quietly whispered, 'And one for you too, Constance Lamal, but later.'

And later, Connie asked him, 'Do you think his father knew Derrick?'

'I have a distinct idea that he did – as I had a small buttercup in my overcoat buttonhole. I had taken several to ensure there was no mistakes and, being quite taken by the whole idea, placed one jauntily as a buttonhole addition – silly, I know, in December, but oddly enough, he, the father, was the only one who gave it more than a second glance. I think he knew and if he didn't then his dear wife would enlighten him. Now, where were we, Connie, in that story of mine you insist I write and you will type?'

'We got up to this moment, Derrick,' and kissed him on the forehead. 'You can talk at the same time as these osculatory gestures,' she said.

'Remind me again of that big word, Connie.'

And she did so willingly.

CHAPTER 3

THE HAPPY GARDENER

'Good evening, H.C.'

'Good evening, Easton. Thank you for dropping in to answer a question. What on Nimbus 9 is Holmes up to these days? I saw him a short time ago emerging from the Archives, a wary smile on his face and arm in arm with his nurse Connie Dickens. They are such a cheerful and hard-working pair. She acts as his secretary/researcher, when he writes; Connie does the typing and printing and the binding of his completed works. And splendid, professional work she makes of it too. Seemingly another vocation, being left behind for the Arts?'

'It looks very much like it, H.C. Has he informed you of his latest work?'

'Yes. Yet another Celestial Request received again ages ago, from a gentleman who wrote articles for newspapers, magazines etc. on gardening subjects. A fine gardener himself he lived in a cottage near Calne, in Wiltshire (South-West Anglo area – as Holmes names it!). His next door neighbour is an elderly, spritely gentleman living on his own, but with domestic help daily. He is an avid gardener a hobby he was advised to take up, following a very traumatic time as a prisoner of war in the Far East.

'The medical authorities were hopeful that such activity, providing it was of not too strenuous a nature, would help put his nightmarish experiences at a distance, and if possible, to complete flight.'

'He has been gently referred to as "simple minded", but has a gentle, kind nature. He lived for a while in the cottage with an aunt – a sister of his dead mother. The aunt died, but left the cottage and a modest legacy of investments made wisely and well in her lifetime.'

'Yes, I'm following you, H.C., and the Request of the gardening expert relating to this gentle man? – Two words used, correctly, I think.'

'Correctly so, Easton. The Request ran as follows. 'I am blessed with a kind, gentleman neighbour, a gardener, like myself who wanders in his garden late at night – sometimes in the small hours. He has never mentioned this habit of his to me although we talk of other things, mostly relating to horticultural affairs we both enjoy. You have been a special friend of mine since I was young, and as you know, I have always wished you well of a night. But shall I open a discussion with him, his name is William, possibly a quiet reference to that lovely flower he grows so well – the Sweet William – a floral nomenclature topic, perhaps, that might lead on to a divulgence of his nocturnal visits to the bottom of his garden. I have never been in his house or his garden, as I have been here for a short while. You have helped me when I had that breakdown, years ago in the Middle East and, often, when I see William, his look of happy bewilderment, reminds me so much of the look facing me in the mirror all those years ago. I am anxious not to disturb the pleasant, undemanding relationship we have, so please advise how I can help William as you once helped me. Bless you, special friend, Happy Gardening, Allen.'

'And naturally, H.C., your advice?'

'I suggested the garden would provide the answer and left it up to him to make the necessary overtures to bring this about.'

'Anything since?'

'No surprisingly, nothing – but I believe Holmes and that creativity of his will find an answer.'

'In story form, of course, H.C.?'

'Naturally, Easton, that's his third string to his bow – a capital investigator, a composer of merit, and with his fair assistant, an author – or should that be plural?'

Allen Wrenfen normally slept soundly, after submitting his customary 200–300 words on the topic he most liked to write about – gardening. It had been a glorious summer, much subject matter for his column and now it was approaching autumn with much work to be done in the potting shed, greenhouse and his not too large an expanse of garden. But on this particular night, when sound sleep escaped him, he left his bed and gazed out at a young moon casting shadows in his garden. One such shadow he recognised at once as his neighbour William Fry. Clad in a dressing gown and slippers, he was walking slowly at the bottom of his garden carrying something nestling in his arms. He then returned empty-handed to his cottage, entered and locked the door.

Wrenfen had seen this activity on the part of his neighbour on several occasions and had pondered deeply as to the reason for such nightly excursions.

He returned to his bed, thought deeply on the matter, and within a short time, captured the former sleep that had escaped him.

He rose, at his usual time 8 a.m. and knew that to solve the matter of the previous night's observation he should endeavour to be asked in by William to discuss garden matters of mutual interest and then be invited into the garden itself.

Rather than making a direct approach to William, he made discreet enquiries as to the carer provided by the Local Authority. Such were speedily made and he established that the carer was a Ms Alison Young, a recently widowed middle-aged lady, with three grown-up children, resident in a flat on the outskirts of the village. In addition to her duties on William's behalf she helped as a volunteer in the local charity shop on behalf of Oxfam. Her attendance hours fitted in adequately with her carer's work, and had seen her occasionally when at home, and, apart from the greeting of the day – usually morning, he had not interrupted her in her carer's mission. He was aware, however of her kind, good looks, her driving skills in her small saloon car, and its sensible parking, neatly reversing into the drive of William's cottage. He should have tried more to develop her acquaintance, but tact and diplomacy were two of his traits in his previous calling as a civil servant. Now he considered, these traits, could be eased a little in furtherance of a good deed. At least, he considered it to be such, he was fully aware of the confidentiality of carer and patient and all the other situations marking such confidences. So, a more delicate method of achieving his aims, he hoped would be by visiting the charity shop in question. At first, on a few occasions, when she was not on duty, and then, having established by careful and discreet observation – second nature to him by his previous security employment with a branch of the civil service, he visited the shop when she was seated at a small desk, itemising small trinkets and items and assessing their possible value before attaching a small sticky label to them. He noticed her puzzled frown when deciding where to attach the label to a small brass swan and then stuck it firmly on its base. He chose a large-print book of *Great Expectations* from the appropriate rack and, when she was free, took it to her.

'Hello, Mr Wrenfen,' she said brightly, 'we meet off duty?'

'We do indeed,' he replied, and proffered the required sum.

'Shall I wrap it for you?' she asked.

'Thank you no; I'll pop it in my shopping bag.' Having paid and placed the book in his bag, he bid her good day and left – no hurried chit-chat or enquiry as to her charge. 'Gently does it,' he thought, like as of old in his previous occupation.

Two days later, following his visit, he casually arranged to meet her as she alighted from her car, to unlatch the gate to the driveway. All so casually arranged, a brief greeting, and a quite unstressed enquiry as to the health of William, and a suggestion that he was always available should there be any heavy lifting tasks in which William needed him – then he, Allen, was always available. 'I'd be awfully pleased if you could let him know, Miss Young.'

'Yes, I'll certainly do that for you – I know he envies your gardening skills and wishes he possessed them.'

'Well, you tell him that I think he is doing well and that his name and Christian name do him great credit.'

'Really, Mr Wrenfen, how?'

'Well, William goes with 'Sweet' (not a dessert of course) and Fry, his surname, is but a contraction of 'friability of the soil' – case explained satisfactorily?'

'Oh yes, I would not have thought of that apposition.'

'I'm sure you would, Miss Young – carer, merely a noun in apposition but a nice one, I think.'

'Disguised flattery, Mr Wrenfen, will get you everywhere.'

'Then I shall try harder next time we meet. Must not hold you up, though – your good deeds await you.'

'So soon another I see!' she said obviously pleased at these gallant expressions.

'Goodbye, Nurse, until our next meeting I hope.'

He left and he saw her park her car, neatly and safely as always – waved lightly to her as he left, but failed to see her return wave, as he turned away.

Another time – arranged visit to the charity shop, another book (again large print) of the *Pickwick Papers*.

A pleasant exchange at the desk counter brought him the news he had so patiently awaited – William would like his help, when possible, in the removal of a tree stump of some width and depth at the far end of the garden – casual working dress – no walking-out uniform required. The allusion to the walking-out uniform intrigued him, indicating he was sure, that William possessed a military background or suchlike.

'Why don't you just pop round and let him know you are both willing and able to help. He'd be delighted, for he often speaks of you and your gardening skills and has often looked for an excuse to meet you – but he knew you were very busy and he had read your articles in *The Daily Press* newspaper. And, I see, a fellow Dickens reader, for sure.'

'You certainly do. It was too obvious really, two books by the same author.'

She smiled, took the exact amount offered and gave him the book and a small receipt adding, 'Just in case you have to bring it back – proof of purchase, as we call it.'

As he went to leave he turned suddenly and slightly bumped into another customer waiting to purchase a framed picture. He apologised to the lady holding the item, and said goodbye to both of them.

'A very polite man, Alison,' said the lady, 'does he visit you often? If so what date and time. I'll be here! I could do with a polite gentleman in my life – too few of them about these days.'

Alison nodded in agreement and thought, 'Yes, but after me, Mrs Cunningham, you're first' – a cheeky thought unspoken of course, but she considered, quite true, 'for there is something about that man, Allen, that I like. I should get to know him better.'

A similar form of musing was engaging Allen's mind as he walked out of the shop. 'Lovely to look at, delightful to know,' now how did the rest of that song go – but it escaped him. He settled for the opening words of this lyric – they would do nicely. And so, unbeknown to each other 'The two parties in question, your honour, proceeded to meet and like each other. A nice phrase to say to the court – wouldn't have gone amiss – what do you think, Connie?' Holmes asked, as he sat back in his chair and handed the written sheets to her for typing.

'Yes, Mr Holmes, but what about the heavy labouring task in the garden?'

'We are progressing slowly in that direction, Connie, and why should it always be a titular Mr Holmes, why not Derrick?'

'I'll try and remember, Mr Holmes, I mean Derrick, and if a cup of tea is called for, just call and I'll make it – agreed, Derrick?'

'Thank you, Connie, yes – but I have meandered. So tomorrow, back to the lathe and see what we can turn out.'

The following day it rained in the early morning, but by early afternoon, it became a pleasant sunny autumnal day – a typical late-summer day in mid-September. Allen noted the arrival of Alison at William's house, and ran its bell a few minutes later. Alison greeted him and complied with William's request to bring him into the sitting room – Alison had already appraised William of Allen's name and so the introduction was a matter of moments, 'Perhaps a cup of tea, coffee, or a little sherry?' William asked.

'A tea would do fine,' Allen returned. Alison needed no first or second bidding and had the electric kettle on in a moment.

'Anything to eat?' queried William, 'a biscuit or two perhaps.'

'Well, that would do comfortably,' he replied, 'as long as I am not outdoing things on my first visit?'

As the three of them took their tea, each in their individual seats with a small table at their side, the conversation soon got down to the 'nitty-gritty facts of the case', as Allen phrased it, and he suggested a spade, fork, crowbar and a sharp-edged saw to be used to sever entangled roots. All such items were to hand in the shed at a corner at the rear of the garden. Refreshments over, Allen followed William along the concrete pathway to the rear of the garden with its offending obstacle awaiting their joint efforts to remove it. As they walked, Allen noticed small garden gnomes sited at about three feet apart on the edges of the pathway – about a dozen in all. He noticed William patted each one as he passed by and heard him murmuring something that sounded like a greeting to each one. Allen thought it odd, but made no comment regarding William's actions. Between them, in a matter of an hour's hard work, the tree trunk was prised from the soil packed solidly about it, and Allen set to work to saw it into manageable lengths for removal.

'It will make good firewood when it dries out a little,' he said to William, who looked so pleased with a mild pleasant air about him. 'A job well done, thank you,' he said simply and kindly.

There was something in his demeanour that attracted Allen and, when later told by Alison, that he had been ill-used and brutally treated by his captors many years ago, William had developed a marked anxiety to please attitude to those who showed him a caring disposition. He is a simple man, bruised mentally and physically but has so many endearing traits. This exchange of confidences occurred between them as they took a stroll in the garden towards evening. Allen found it pleasant to be in her company as they walked and talked aware that he liked her undemanding ways.

He saw how caring she was with William, her charge, gently but firmly putting things to right whenever he mislaid his writing materials, he required immediately to write one of his letters to authority, as he called them.

'Official ones?' queried Allen.

'Well, yes and no. They always concern his bête noire.'

'And that is?' returned Allen.

'You won't laugh, will you?' she replied.

'Of course not,' he said, 'this is in strict confidence, is it not?'

'Well, the letters relate to his garden gnomes – to all of whom he has given names, and a kind of community history.'

'Odd but understandable, I suppose, we lonely folk must have someone to talk to on occasion, if it's only a morning greeting or such. And the correspondence concerned his family of?' he queried.

'Twelve,' she replied – 'and his letters are always directed to The Chief Authority, The Royal Horticultural Society, Chelsea, London SW1. They are always the same, courteously phrased, pointing out that since the RHS was established in 1805, it had not allowed ornamental items to intervene with its floral displays and Chelsea Flower Show in May each year was the poorer for it.'

William had researched the history of gnomes, previously made as earthenware figurines and he avows that gnomes possess powers of protection for their caring owners. Apparently, his aunt, just before her death believing in such powers, purchased the gnomes and as she lay dying, told her favourite and only nephew, that they would always be there to protect him from the vicissitudes of life. It was part of her legacy to him, including the cottage etc. that he values most.

'A charming and salutary tale,' Allen returned, 'but what of his written representations on behalf of gnomes to the authorities at the RHS?'

'Always the same – to be deplored as detracting from floral beauty and its display potential.'

'And his reaction? – does he take it badly?'

'Not at all, it is not in his disposition to take offence

– he merely goes to the bottom of his garden, carrying a couple of his gnomes and explains the situation to them. He told me this in confidence one day on receiving yet another negative reply to his request.'

As Alison said the last word, Allen's thoughts went back to the request he had made earlier to his Special Friend, and knew instantly that it had been granted, and was aware of the help he would be able to give to a simple-minded kind soul of a neighbour.

'Our secret, Allen,' she said when they parted later that evening.

'Mum's the word,' he replied jovially.

'It had better be,' she said, 'otherwise . . .' but did not finish the sentence.

'Otherwise what?' he pursued.

'You know that already,' she replied.

'I thought you had not noticed,' he replied.

'Never discount a woman's intuition, Allen.'

'I hope it's favourable!'

'It could easily be so, don't you agree?'

'It shall have my profoundest thoughts, Alison – may I ring you about them?'

'Please do. Goodnight, Allen.'

'Goodnight, Alison. Thank you for all you do for William,' – a pause, 'and me too,' he said. 'A safe journey home,' he added as she entered her car and drove slowly, he thought, away.

The following day he visited the same charity shop, ostensibly to see Alison, but since she was not on duty, browsed through the shelves, saw a small brass kettle with handle and lid, asked its price, £1.99, bought it and took it home. The kettle stood around two to three inches high, was brightly polished and he knew to what use it could be put. When in the garden previously with Alison, he had seen tucked away neatly on a shelf in the garden shed, a small china tea service with a small brightly coloured teapot. He saw a few crumbs on one of the small plates, suggestive that a biscuit or something similar had been part of a tea party of sorts.

The following evening, having written his weekly article, he pieced together his observation and came to the conclusion that when dusk, William had taken perhaps several of his gnomes to the bottom of the garden, set out the small cups etc. and held a simple tea party during which he spoke about the cruel negative reply to his letters on their behalf.

He deeply sympathised with William's strange behaviour, though he knew its original source by treating the gnomes as the substitutes for his previous barbaric guards when a prisoner of war and talking to them as fellow human beings with no necessity to resort to violent, inhuman behaviour. The more he thought of this possibility of William's efforts to put right his experience of man's utter inhumanity to man, the more his sympathies were aroused on William's behalf.

His writing finished he put the small kettle in his jacket pocket. When he saw William in the garden – not quite knowing why he smeared a little earth on the kettle and holding it up over the dividing fence remarked:

'Hello, William, look what I found.'

William looked at the item and a slow smile crept over his face. 'What are you going to do with it?' he asked pointedly – obviously interested in the find.

'I thought of giving it to some child to go with a tea set – what do you think?'

'Well, I wouldn't mind having it, Allen – if you don't mind, that is.'

'Well, what about a quid pro quo then? Alison told me you write a lot to the RHS about a project of yours – may I help? Writing is much in my line, as you know?'

William's smile grew broader. 'It's a deal,' he said

warmly. Allen handed him the small item knowing full well of the eventual use by William, and then said, 'Just let me know when you need my discreet and tactful help and I'll come along.'

They took leave of each other and Allen noticed William carrying the new-treasured item into his shed. That night, he took down from his bookshelf two booklets one by Ronald Sayle (a former POW) and one by Eminent Academic (Knight of the Bushido) and browsed through their pages just to refresh his memory on their contents, read in depth previously. He, himself had been too young to have taken part in that bitter ill-fought war long ago, but was aware of the debt that civilisations owed to those (then young men) like William, who miles away from their homeland fought to put things right – as William put it in his letter to the RHS authorities.

As a gardening correspondent, and well versed in the written terms of acceptability by those in high places, he considered his course of action.

The campaign he envisaged fighting if necessary on William's behalf was simple. It was based on altering the views that had prevailed for some 208 years regarding the non-acceptance of new plastic brightly coloured garden gnomes in the annual flower display between 21 and 25 May each year.

With the aid of a charming colleague, a journalist of some skill and persuasion, he amassed the intelligence she gathered on gnomes and their antecedent history. Apparently, many attempts had been made by interested parties throughout the country to persuade the RHS to end their discriminatory attitude towards garden gnomes and the ilk (pixies, leprechauns, fairies etc.) being part of floral displays at the Chelsea Flower Show, but all to no avail.

The seventeen-member council were all members of the

Human Race – had their foibles, weaknesses and strengths – but how best to cause them to alter their views on the heated discussion on the attendance of garden gnomes for but five days a year at the annual flower show? He had no doubt that it would not be an easy task – many had tried and failed to end the discrimination shown to non-verbal garden ornaments who could not speak on their own behalf.

The letter he eventually composed and sent in William's name stressed the long-held hopes of a simple man – disturbed in mind as a direct result of his barbaric treatment at the hands of his inhuman captors, his love of gardening and its well-known benefits to mental and physical health; emphasis on their compassion as fellow garden lovers (each and every one of them race, gender, creed, notwithstanding) and lastly drawing their attention to the recently drawn-up covenants between the country and its armed forces, given great publicity by the current Prime Minister – also if a precedent worries them, think of the recent U-turn on recognition of Arctic Heroes as they were called (long after the death of many of them) by the covenant on the few survivors, an arctic medal. His last lines read, 'There are so few left of those to whom we owe our present way of life. The ages of garden gnomes are indeterminate but surely we owe to them an acceptance into our floral ranks.' If you could only reply to William Fry that his Request has been seriously considered and he will be notified as speedily as possible of the results of your deliberations, it would make a brave and simple man extremely happy. We take from this world only that which we give away, so do please endeavour to give his Request a sympathetic hearing and show compassion. After all, we owe a great debt to him and many men like him (so few left, alas) for their unselfish efforts on our behalf so many, many years ago.

'Yours most sincerely, Allen Wrenfen (Gardening Correspondent, *The Daily Press*).'

Now, Mr Derrick Holmes, how do you propose to end this story?' asked his carer.

'Well, Connie,' he replied, 'this is where your feminine touch comes into play. I noticed in the story that Alison referred to her woman's intuition; might it not relate to those charity shop visits of Allen, in order to further their friendship? I think even then she knew such visits were for a purpose he was unaware of at the time.'

'I think you are probably right, Mr Holmes, I mean Derrick, for she is undoubtedly fond of him.'

Dear Mr William Fry,

I must first apologise for our flagrant display of discrimination over many years (including of course all those relating to your correspondence to us) against garden gnomes and suchlike, being part of the annual floral display at the Chelsea Flower Show.

I am extremely pleased to say that the display this year between 21 and 25 May, garden gnomes will be considered as acceptable garden ornaments, and as such will be deemed to enhance the importance of the Royal Horticultural Display. May I also say the seventeen-member council wish me to extend their thanks to you and so many others who have suggested the views we now hold on this protected species. It was the considered opinion of all seventeen council members that not only a sense of humour should prevail but also compassion. I was once asked by a small blind girl, at one of our floral events, as she stood near a glorious display of flowers and felt their leaves tremble in a light breeze, 'What colour was the wind?' I looked at this young beautiful child, as her blank eyes met mine, and but for a microsecond, thought of a possible answer and then said, 'What colour would you like it to be?'

'Well,' she said, 'Mummy often says to me on my birthday and at Christmas, Roses are red, violets are blue, we've saved our pennies and bought this for you, and then I get a lovely present – so could it be blue?'

'For you, young lady, it will be ever blue,' I replied and I am sure my eyes were blurred as much as those of her parents standing beside her. Today I still wonder how out of all the people, she chose me, a person she could not see, to ask for an answer to her question. I can but suggest that such children, even pets, and possibly garden gnomes, know instinctively those who love them. Thank you so much, William (please overlook the informality of this latter salutation), for your kind letters over the years.

With the warmest of wishes, yours most sincerely,
Charles Hardie.

The insistent buzzing of his front doorbell interrupted Allen in his study, busily writing his article on garden matters, and other correspondence. On opening the door he saw both William and Alison smiling broadly, and each wanting to be the first to tell him of the receipt of the letter from the RHS. He invited them in at once, and after reading the letter, insisted on a small drink of whatever (as he called it) to celebrate the occasion.

Refreshments accepted all round, they talked of the possibility of acquiring tickets to attend the flower show the following year. William was in full agreement with the suggestion and wondered if he might take one of his gnomes, site it secretly in a floral display, have a discreet photo of the three of us admiring it, surely a bystander (a garden lover of course and perhaps a gnome owner) would oblige by taking the photo.

'I have never seen William so utterly content and happy,' remarked Alison to Allen as they helped William back to his cottage. Allen then went to return to his home, but before leaving, said to Alison, 'Might you be able to call in before you leave later? I shall be on my best behaviour as your host but only if you have the time of course. If not, perhaps on some other occasion?' Alison looked at this diffident, unsure of himself man, as she thought that if there was to be a close friendship, she would cause it to happen, and merely said, 'Now perhaps, Allen?'

'Why not, Alison,' he said briskly, 'may I take your coat?' and did so briskly, all diffidence gone in an instant.

CHAPTER 4

A MIDSUMMER'S DAYDREAM

'Good morning, H.C.'

'Greetings of this lovely day to you, Easton – you have that 'news of Holmes' look about you. Are you going to apprise me of his recent activities?'

'Correct, H.C., he has discovered a Celestial Request recently received from a daughter whose mother was in the Special Intensive Care (SIC) ward of a small hospital near Bristol (South-West Anglo area, as Holmes styles it). Thanks to the devoted hospital staff, her mother recovered from a spinal fusion operation that had taken place in a private hospital nearby. Her mother had been close to death, a cardiac arrest of some duration. But the skill of the hospital staff in the SIC ward saved her.

'The daughter has learnt that this small but wonderfully staffed hospital is earmarked for closure. It has a wonderful history of care for all in its immediate vicinity and also has accepted casualties conveyed by helicopter, from other areas. The suggested closure is believed to have been caused by the current harsh economic difficulties pertaining to that country. The Request is that might something be done to obviate the need for the closure of the hospital whose staff over a long period has given loyal and skilled service to all their patients?

'Apparently some Celestial help was promised and Holmes has taken it upon himself to rectify and improve the situation in his own inimitable way.'

'And that being, Easton?'

'His efficient secretary/carer has been busy on his behalf obtaining all details available concerning the Cenotaph, designed by Edwin Lutyens and erected in Whitehall, London, in 1920. It was to be a National Memorial in memory of all those killed in the Great War for Civilisation in 1914–1919, and of course similar horrific casualties in other subsequent conflicts.'

'Yes, Easton, I've always known Holmes as "a peace-lover extraordinaire" and he does so much to put "his Speck of Dust" to rights by abolishing all warlike activity among the nations and what is his research aimed at on this occasion?'

'He is aware that his suggestion for the removal of the Cenotaph will be the subject of much resistance, but as he says, he has done his homework and it is to be replaced by a modern hospital for children to be situated in a country location near Bristol (South-West Anglo area) – a far more useful memorial than lifeless stone.'

'Yes, Easton, I am sure there are many people holding similar views to his, but the resistance to his plan will come from many quarters.'

'Yes, he agrees that will happen, but he has assessed the weight of the Portland stone used in its construction as weighing about 120 tons, say nearly 269,000 lb.'

'Is the weight a necessary part of his calculations?'

'Indeed it is, as he proposes to use it in the manufacture of smaller stone versions of the monument. They are to be of a weight ranging from ¾ lb to 1 lb and suitably inscribed with words other than "The Glorious Dead". He feels there is nothing glorious about being dead. It is better to live, love, laugh and have no necessity to go to war. And I agree with him, and I'm certain my views are shared by many.

'His financial calculations, involving cost of manufacture, presentation caskets, envisage a sale direct and/or by auction, to a worldwide clientele. Particularly in the dominions whose casualties included 1,081,952 killed in the Great War.

'Assuming 268,800 lb of stone would be produced and allowing for wastage during the manufacturing process, he estimates that at £10 per item cost it would produce about £26,000,000 considerably more if the 1 lb weight of the item were reduced to ¾, or even ½ lb. He has taken into consideration postage and packing costs in respect of overseas purchases, and hopes that re-employed staff would be engaged in various stages of the production, distribution etc.

'He hopes also to interest the government to donate a sum comparable to that raised. He even has in mind a lottery donation of no mean order. The site for the National Memorial Hospital for Children is no problem, he states, for there is the one earmarked for closure in the Anglo South-West area, namely the one mentioned earlier.

'If needs be reconstruction work could be put into effect and if well staffed and well equipped, that could become the National Memorial Hospital. If not so used, then the hospital in question could be demolished and the suggested National Memorial Hospital takes its place. He believes that all future memorials should be in the form of aids to the living, to the sick, the elderly, the young, those disabled mentally or physically, the blind and those with impaired vision. Trusts set up for the training of would-be doctors and nurses, healers, social workers, carers – he'll have a list a mile long of those for whom his sympathies lie.'

'So typical of Holmes, Easton, if ever a heart was in its right place, his is. I know he feels that so much hypocrisy is associated with these memorials and remembrance days – all remembering for but a short time and then all speedily forgotten. Uniforms, swords, decorations, medals, and other insignia put away for another year. He has mentioned this to me on many occasions – 'Widowhood is twelve months long – not half a day.' He has many such views and not at all backward in making them known.'

'Well, Easton, on a day such as this, I think Holmes is entitled to daydream – but, who knows, dreams have come true – especially on our Nimbus 9.'

'My one once did, thanks to you, H.C.'

'Shall I see you in a bit, Easton, as they say in Cornwall, so I'm told?'

'Of course, H.C., I wouldn't miss it!'

CHAPTER 5

DECEPTION PLAN B

'Good morning, H.C., alfresco reading today?' said Charles Easton noticing the sheaf of papers perused by his companion.

'Oh, hello, Easton, the top of the morning to you! I've always loved that greeting, it betokens a beautiful day such as this is about to unfold. If you are not too busy, would you care to join me? Room enough for two on this my favourite bench.'

'Willingly, H.C., the red tape binding your papers suggests it is one of Holmes' briefs, as he calls his Celestial Requests stories?'

'Yes, it is one such and based on a Request we received during that last terrible war. It was but one of many received at that time.'

'And Holmes has developed it with his usual flair, no doubt?'

'Yes. The Request related to a young army officer's problem. He intended to write a spoof story, as he called it, on the decision of the top brass to order an attack that had no hope of a successful result – it being hastily mounted with very little artillery and tank support. Among the very heavy casualties sustained, were many of his close and loyal friends. Theirs was a Dominion Brigade with a scarcity of reinforcements as replacements. It had been involved in heavy fighting in Crete in May/June of the previous year involving a depletion of its strength. The young man thought that by writing a spoof story relating to the High Command's incompetence, as he thought it, it would help release some of the anger and sorrow within him. But he wondered if in so writing it might cast aspersions on the officer corps as a whole, or reflect badly on them in any way.'

'A release valve, so to speak, I suppose, H.C.? Lots of us resort to such things in stressful situations. But since his story was not for publication, it would be merely a personal matter . . . did his Request receive such a suggested answer?'

'Yes. He was told to sleep on it and eventually he wrote an amusing tale very short, but, Holmes, that powerhouse of a peace lover, has, he thinks, improved it with due apologies to all concerned; the officer corps, the clergy, but not those possessing warlike tendencies.'

'Typically our Holmes of course, H.C. – he has always hated the books on war and their hate-filled chapters. I notice you have finished reading it. May I borrow it?'

'Yes, Easton, by all means, I think you will find he has provided a humorous touch or two to the denunciation of aggressive warlike activity. I was tempted to refer to Voltaire and his book *Candide* which is stark writing on the futility of war, that was published and seemingly, the friendship between Voltaire and Frederic the Great did not suffer immediately. Fred the Great, he used to call him – but not in his hearing or presence, at Sans Souci – Fred's place, as he styled it – a pity though that 1870 led to 1914–1940. A ridiculous case of causus bellum over some sprig of royalty earmarked for a regal position in a country other than his own. But then most conflicts stem from strange events – so costly and wasteful too.'

'In many ways, H.C., in many ways.'

'There is no rush for the return of the file, Easton. Shall I expect you this evening?'

'But of course, H.C. – wouldn't miss our get-togethers discussing the problems of Holmes's Speck of Dust. I'm sure I shall enjoy the mischievous views of D. Holmes Esq.!'

The story (NB: Spoof – see OE Dictionary): (1) Special Piece of Ordinary Foolscap (2) Or army jargon among other ranks . . . 'taking the Michael'.

The title: Deception – Plan B.

'Yes, what is it, Gerald?'

'I'm sorry to butt in like this, Colonel, but I think that the new Lieutenant Smiles who joined the battalion in the UK just before we left for the Middle East, has broken down and reached his limit of endurance.'

'What do you mean, Gerald?'

'It is about the attack we are to put in tonight – another 'show' as Higher Authority calls it.'

'And, Gerald, what has happened?'

'Lieutenant Smiles has assembled his platoon around him and is addressing them in biblical terms.'

'In what terms?'

'He opened his briefing for the attack in the following way: "Dearly beloved platoon and fellow soldiers, we are gathered here this evening in the sight of God to attack and kill fellow human beings wearing apparel and helmets different from our own. Before the attack you will all take nourishment – the staff of life, bread and five small fishes."'

'This is ridiculous, Gerald. Surely the senior NCOs are not party to this nonsense?'

'On the contrary, Colonel; they, and the entire platoon, think it is highly original – having been "put in the picture" before – a phrase greatly used by the top brass on similar occasions when an attack is to be made.'

'Oh, perhaps it is just a jest – an amusing opening to the customary briefing? A passing fancy, perhaps? As you know, he is an Oxford man and did well at El Alamein as most of the young officers did in that ten-day battle.'

'I hope you are right, Colonel, but he refers to raiment instead of battledress, ploughshares instead of personal firearms and the field-dressing pack as an additional method of mercy. Any stragglers in the proposed mighty onslaught – his words – would have to make atonement to enable their sins to be forgiven (Platoon Sergeant to note please).'

'But this is highly irregular behaviour on the part of a junior officer, Gerald. Why did you not step in and intervene in some tactful way?'

'It was my intention to do so, Colonel, but I found it so amusingly original, that I wondered if it had been officially sanctioned by the fire-eating, wrathful general officer commanding our division.'

'God forbid, Gerald, but it is as you say intriguing and original . . . what happened next?'

'You mean after his briefing?'

'Yes.'

'It is still going on, Colonel. It has got them all spellbound – his belief in the justice of his cause, as he names it. "No killing of the enemy. They are to be slain according to the wisdom of Almighty Authority that shall not be spoken of lightly if ever at all, until after the war itself is finished and we all answer at the huge peace table in Holyrood Palace Garden on a rainy day with a benign breeze afoot."'

'This is getting quite ridiculous, Gerald – do go on.'

'He refers to the positive fortifications of the enemy lines as being many mansions to be destroyed, if it were not so ordered he would not be talking about it. And some of our artillery shells will not flourish in supporting us, if they fall astray and become unfriendly. He had taken steps, he added, to liaise with the gunner officers to put aside any ammunition likely to be unfriendly. They would all advance as a host under a thunderous barrage and gradually our good works would be made known to the enemy and greatly astonish them. All prisoners (if any) will be fed and watered – the usual army rations of course – before being taken to a place where they will all dwell until hostilities worldwide cease. In addition to personal arms, a rod and staff will be provided to all concerned to comfort them if wounded and have to wait medical attention. This coverage is not temporary, it will cover them all the days of their life when, eventually, their military service finishes.'

'How did you manage to record all this, Gerald?'

'I taped it, Colonel, on one of those appliances recently issued to all second-in-commands of battalions.'

'Amazing! Do put in an indent for me later – but do continue, Gerald. This is beginning to remind me of my schooldays, Sunday church and all that.'

'Yes it does rather bring those memories back to life. I thought this deviation from the normal way of briefing troops before battle would interest you, Colonel. He also made brief reference to lots being cast after the battle for enemy items of memorabilia. But intelligence bits must go back to top brass to help them in their plans.'

'It gets so interesting, Gerald. So, so different from the briefing we were taught at Sandhurst.'

'Yes, and don't forget the manual of infantry training etc.'

'Yes of course. This is really strange. And you say it is still going on now, Gerald?'

'Well, to tell you the truth, cards on the table and all that, it isn't and has not taken place at all.'

'What! And why this news then?'

'Just a joke, Colonel – it is after all April the 1st, All Fools' Day, and believe me or not, Colonel, we are all fools being here to slaughter each other in wretchedly callous ways. How many years has this up-and-down desert battle been going on? You win, I lose – you don't win, I don't lose attitude to life. In five days' time we shall have another battle on our hands just as awful as that one in Egypt in late October last year, and somehow, I don't think I'll get through this next battle . . . I honestly believe my days are numbered and I shall dwell in that fabled house for ever and ever.'

'Don't be such a fool, Gerald! Of course you won't be a casualty. I'll make certain of that.'

'How, Colonel?'

'I'll recommend you for a home posting – your four years out here without a break is long enough for a tour of duty overseas.'

'Thank you, Colonel, I know I could do with a break.'

Later, that evening in a letter written to his wife – Major Gerald Fortune informed her of his eventual home posting – 'No dates given of course but expect me soon.'

Mrs Dorothy Fortune on its receipt, turned to her father a retired general of infantry and said, 'Thank you, Daddy. It worked as you said it would.'

'Yes, my dear, it did for me once in India when I had to serve under an arrogant commanding officer, highly disliked by all.'

'And Daddy?'

'I got pushed upstairs because it was said I was a "nutcase" and had stood too close to the sun. It was easy to get sunstroke in India and a short break in a hill station – Deolali was recommended – hence the phrase "doolally tap" became applicable. After all, the overseas tours then lasted seven long years.'

'Do you think, Daddy, they will twig it in Gerald's case?'

'No, my dear, not if the War Office is the same as it was in my day.'

'Let's hope so and I pray it is so.'

'Steady, my child, no more praying at present, leave that to Gerald – he is only using the system and it does pay to keep sane in the long run.'

'You are probably right, Daddy. But a short prayer won't hurt, will it?'

'It never does, my dear.'

In the field

Subject: recovered documents.

To: Lt Col. Geoffrey Dorchester, OBE, sir, the attached papers were found in a rubbish receptacle near the officers' quarters recently vacated by Major Gerald Fortune, MC – shortly after his home posting to the United Kingdom.

Since the heading referred to pre-attack briefing, I thought they should be referred to you. I have pro tem, given them a "secret" classification, but you may wish to amend this to "top secret" as if such documents were to fall into enemy hands, we as a unit, might become a laughing stock or even worse – Respectfully submitted, C. E. Pugh, Capt., Regt. Padre.

GUIDANCE NOTES
FOR PRE-ATTACK BRIEFING

Well, fellow attackers, I have had words with our supporting artillery commander and have entreated him to select unfriendly-looking shells and cause these to fall mightily upon the enemy host. You may recall the panic their friendly fire caused us in the last attack we made. Quite scary it was.

I thought we might have a few verses of that lovely Jewish family song 'Abey, Abey, My Boy' to sing as we plod up to the start line. Most of you know the words and if we can get one of our buglers to play it, it will provide uplifting fervour we do need so desperately in these constant attacks. Thank goodness we are proceeding westwards in a homeward direction. Anyway, here are the song words, just jot them down if you like.

> Abey, Abey, my boy,
> Vot are ve voting for now?
> All the family
> Keep on asking me
> Vitch day, vot day,
> I don't know vot to say,
> Abey, Abey, my boy,
> Vot are ve vaiting for now?

You can of course make up other verses as you go along to suggest Abey should marry the girl and not keep her vaiting, I mean waiting.

Oh, another thing. The top brass dislike our referring to the enemy commander as "Heiny" his full rank and name are to be used at all times when referring to his undoubted military skills and whatnot. So, from hence and now on, it will be General Heinrich Dom and Blasstoff. Don't worry about his decorations as there are about three rows and even I can't remember them all. I tried once to commit them all to memory. Let me think now. Black Cross Order of the White Horse, Steel Cross, Westphalian Service Medal with Chivalry Bar, Long Service Medal for Service in Cold Stations (that's not railway ones of course), Swabian Duelling Order 2nd Class, and many others for gallant conduct – but, as I say, far too many to refer to. I still call him "Heiny" myself. It is easier to remember. After the battle lots will be cast for any raiment or items of loot particularly of interest to the top brass. I think that is all for the present. If in the attack anything else comes to mind, we shall halt and I will complete the briefing . . . well, good luck to us one and all (and in an aside to your platoon sergeant ask: 'And how did you think it went, Sergeant?').

'He will say (having been told previously what his reply is to be), "It went down very well, sir. Far better than last time when we could not hear all what was said because of the thunder of the guns – the sound of the argument of kings – as explained to us."'

'Yes I think it was that dreadful noise – a veritable cacophony of strident sound, as you called it. They never told us that at Sandhurst about briefing troops under clamorous situations. I've a good mind to write to the commandant to be considered as a synopsis of differences between briefings in active and non-active stations – I shall send it uncensored of course.'

'Do you think that wise, sir?'

'Now, Sergeant, we must not be flippant!'

'Yes, you're right, sir, sorry.'

'Well, off we jolly well go. Then I'll take the lead, as usual, and you follow. And it's not a dance. This is war, dangerous stuff, no joke about it. And other ad-lib remarks of not too humorous a nature if and only if (nota bene) they are warranted and won't mar the seriousness of the briefing.

(These guidance notes should only be referred to when absolutely necessary and one's at the end of one's tether). But don't destroy before reading and usage. Oh, and good luck.'

CHAPTER 6

IN THE EVENT OF ANY EVENTUALITIES

It had been yet another glorious sunny day at Headquarters Nimbus 9 as the late afternoon sun sank slowly below the southern horizon. It was the favourite time of H.C. to take, as he called it, his garden constitutional walk. He saw his Minister for Enquiries and Requests, Charles Easton, approaching.

'Good evening, Easton! Care to join me?'

'With great pleasure, H.C. I notice you are smiling, an amusing Nimbus 9 recollection perhaps?'

'Yes. Earlier, I met up with Holmes and his delightful carer/nurse, both admiring as usual, the orchids, scene of his early retirement as your Chief Investigations Officer, perhaps?'

'Possibly, H.C., but how do you think he is progressing after his heart attack?'

'Slowly but surely, and as ever, anxious to keep that creative mind of his fully engaged. He has completed his *Butterfly Ballet* sequel, and I attended his first rehearsal. It is very promising. I was greatly impressed. But he now has in mind to develop a story based on a Celestial Request I received many years ago from a young boy named Robert. As you know, Easton, a detailed log is kept on all C.R.'s received, but I prefer to use the full title "Celestial Requests Mentioned in Despatches" – abbreviations are so profuse these days.'

'I agree, H.C.'

'There you are, Easton – an immediate faux pas almost!'

'Touché but what has he in mind? A biographical fragment – a novel or one of his so interesting plots, with an unexpected final chapter?'

'I don't know exactly, Easton, but I know he has been delving into the Archives with his carer/helper. It should be interesting whatever he has in mind. Will I see you later this evening?'

'But of course, I am delighted to be invited. Anything special you would like me to bring? Daily occurrence log, perhaps?'

'No, just you, Easton, and Jess (my granddaughter) and her companion will be there, so we might be four for whist, even bridge? We could just chat, if card games are not to your taste?'

'The usual nightcap, H.C.?'

'But of course. Goodbye, Easton.'

'Goodbye, H.C.'

'I rather like this one, Nurse,' said Holmes to his companion, as he passed to her the Request he had extracted from the C.R. Archives. Nurse Constance Dickens took it from him and read:

Burns, Robert, Referencing No. CR/22/43

Dear Special Person and my friend,

You know I told you about my little hamster, Hammy, who died of old age and my dad had to bury him in our garden in a small shoebox my sister Margaret gave me? Well, my dad said you might be able to give him a warm soul again and you could send him to another boy or girl who would look after him like I did. I would like him to go to a nice friendly home where he could run about on a settee or even a sofa, to get his little legs stretched – like we do when my dad said,

'We'll go out and stretch our legs a bit.' I think it helps me grow a bit for the pencil mark on the kitchen door has gone up a bit. My dad said one day I will be tall enough for a Guardsman, but I want to drive the train and not be at the back.

I'm sorry I couldn't give you the diet for Hammy last night as I had to have a bath from the mud playing football in the garden, but I am all clean and like a shipshape now as I am talking to you as a special person and my friend. I am on packed lunches at school now.

Love to you all and Hammy,
Robert.

PS. I am to have another hamster for my birthday – perhaps a lady one. I can call her Milly – you can tell Hammy if you like. He won't mind because he likes lady hamsters. My dad told me and he is always right.

More love,
Robert.

Much, much later:

Dear Social Person and my friend.

It was many years ago when I was young and small when we used to have those little chats. I am sorry that as I grew up I forgot you. It is nearly ten o'clock at night here in the desert near a small unused railway station named El Almein. It is a dark night and all around the slit trench I am in are other similar trenches holding all the men of my platoon. We have been in these trenches since nightfall yesterday evening in order to conceal signs of our attack on an enemy I have never seen. There are shapes everywhere, tanks, lorries, trucks, tin cans with lamps in them marking tracks we must follow to our starting point. The barrage from 882 guns has started – noise, dust, flares, searchlights to mark courses to our objectives beyond the shell-lit horizon.

We move forward and I am afraid of showing fear – but I have a splendid platoon sergeant and well-trained men and I know with your help I can set a good example to my men – do take care of them for me, for I shall be too busy making sure we are in the right direction and close to our barrage.

You are still my Special Person and my friend, you know,
    Robert.

'I think that is the last Request in this file, Nurse, and now it is for me to link these to the theme of the story I have in mind.'

'No, Mr Holmes, I've found this Request under the same surname, but with Alistair instead of Robert as the Christian name.'

Holmes took the small item and read:

Dear Special Friend wherever you are –

I am not a religious man, but look after Robert for us. He was our only son and we miss him so much. When he was small I told him about that Special Friend he always had. I thought then that I had made it up as a story, but I know now so differently – thank you.

Robert's dad, Alistair, and family.

'Thank you, Nurse Constance Dickens. Your young eyes are obviously better than mine in delving in all this paperwork!'

'I think, Mr Holmes, that as your long-term carer, I might just become Nurse Constance?'

'I agree, and I'll go one better. Might Nurse Connie be acceptable as we are to be co-authors in this undertaking – and Mr Holmes will do me fine. It's agreed then? Now, as to the development of the theme, it would appear from that last recorded Request – and quite a tough one that, too – that Robert did not survive that battle he referred to

– or, because of the difference in the dates of his and his father's Requests, namely October 1942 and April 1943, a further battle occurred in which he lost his life. Thanks to you finding that last Request of his father, I think I can make a sensitive attempt at threading this sad tale together. When it eventually develops in the way I have in mind, I shall rely on you for those feminine touches so essential in a well-told tale such as I hope this to become.

Dear Sir,

I am directed by the General Officer Commanding 5th Highland Division, to inform you of the death of your son, Robert Charles Burns, who was killed in action on the 6th April 1943. He was a fine young officer, extremely efficient and so well liked by all ranks in his Division. His bravery in all our actions since late October 1942 has been made the subject of a recommendation for outstanding bravery. It is our mutual hope at this Division that he will be awarded a decoration for his loyal services to his country.

We extend to you, Sir, our deepest sympathy in your loss – we know our Division will grieve his loss just as deeply as those at home.

I understand that a personal item of your son's was entrusted to his platoon sergeant Angus MacDonald to send or convey to you when circumstances permit.

I personally knew your son, from the day he joined the Barracks of the 5/7th Gordon Highlanders just before we left the UK for the Middle East. He proved to be a true, loyal and brave comrade whom I shall greatly miss.

Yours sincerely and sympathetically,
Robert Hughes, Officer Commanding 5/7th Gordon Highlanders, MEE, APO 151

Dear Mr Burns, Sir

As the Platoon Sergeant of No. 12 Platoon, 'C'Company, 5/7th Battalion the Gordon Highlands, of which your son Lieutenant Robert Burns was the commander, I write to extend to you my deepest and truest sympathy at the loss of your son.

I have, as a former seasoned regular soldier, known many officers and gentlemen, but your son outshone them all. I use the word in its truest sense, but your son was really loved and respected by not only every member of his Platoon, but by the entire company. Although young in years, he was wise, kind, compassionate and very, very efficient as a platoon commander. Although firm on occasions when such firmness was warranted, he exercised his responsibility for the safety and welfare of us all, in an exemplary way. He set us all a fine example of what a real officer in the British Armed Forces should be. I fought alongside him in several battles – always to his right – a pace or two behind him (as he stipulated once when I went in front of him, 'Sergeant Macdonald, now who is leading this platoon, you or . . . ?' He left it unsaid, for although he called me once his 'right-hand man' I stepped back to my usual place.

When he was awarded his 2nd PIP to become a full lieutenant the entire platoon was delighted for he had earned it both in and out of battle, it seems odd to say it, but he, at his young age, became my 2nd mentor and I think, I became a far better and wiser platoon sergeant for it.

Had he lived and made the army his calling/profession, he would have soared in those red-banded ranks. I hope indeed I know, in my innermost heart, that I was more to him than his senior platoon NCO – I think I was his friend – always respectful, dutifully complying with requirements of the unspoken class-structured situation, I knew him to be what I was to him a real friend.

51

He died bravely as a true, worthy and faithful servant of his country.

I enclose with this letter, the wristwatch he asked me once to see was returned to you, as he put it, 'in the event of any eventualities, Sergeant MacDonald, you understand?'

I know, Sir, that you and your wife miss him so much and I miss him, too – and I am not his father, but I wish one day to have a son of my own like him. And he, too, will have the name Robert. If this letter of sincere condolence should prove a little lengthy for such a purpose, I apologise. But one day I hope to write more about my young platoon commander and hope to do fuller justice to his memory.

I remain, Sir, yours most sincerely and sorrowfully,
Angus MacDonald.

PS. Should you wish to contact me on any matter relating to your son – I am at present at General Hospital, Ward 7 APO 467, Hants. Tel 0127344299.

PPS. I have enclosed a small account of the last major battle we fought in North Africa – the war ending in that theatre of operations about one month later in early May 1943.

A.M.
Sgt MacDonald

'Sir.'

'Gather the platoon around me and I'll give them the "low down" on this attack we are to put in.'

'As good as done, sir.'

When the platoon was assembled as he requested, he continued, 'This attack will be at night so as to catch the enemy on the wrong foot.'

'That will be the day, sir,' murmured Pte Campbell, the smallest in the platoon at 5' 2".

'Quiet, Campbell,' – hissed Sgt MacDonald.

'Sorry, sir.'

'Right, we go in just after dusk – the usual barrage will support us right up to the enemy wire and beyond, if needed. We, as part of 'C' Company, will be in the lead 'A' and 'B' Companies to our left and to our right flank – so we are in good, experienced company. You all know the rules. The usual two section corporals Menzies and Muir in charge. No bunching, same space drill we've always used – Bren gunners well to the fore – ready to go into action and return fire once enemy fire tracer or muzzle burst indications are located – usual grenade 38 Mills – two belts of ammunition – water bottle filled, field dressings as per norm, small packs only – this is not a field service marching order walkover – this will be a tough one – a bit like El Alamein, perhaps – and we all know how tough that was.'

'Hear! hear!' Again Campbell being the culprit, but pleasantly ignored by all senior ranks who knew that, like the Lieutenant, he spoke the truth about that ten-day-long battle with over 1,500 casualties a day.

'I think that's all – the usual enemy of course – Italians and Germans, the usual Afrika Korps tough nuts – but not so many of them this time. Right, any questions?'

They all knew the score – had grabbed a meal of sorts before moving up into line along a range of low hills – in front of which rose the heights of the enemy positions.

Cigarette tins as full as stocks provided – matches in safe waterproof areas, bootlaces firmly tied, field dressings bulging slightly from battledress trousers. Water bottle corks firmly fixed, bayonets yet to be affixed, and anything likely to come astray tightened. Then came the usual infantry soldiers' deliberate pre-battle routine – avoid looking at the stretcher-bearers but inwardly glad they are present, rolled groundsheet for inclement weather, not greatly used in the long desert behind them over 1,000 miles of it and pleased to leave it behind and to be proceeding in the direction homewards to the west.

The usual banter, hiding nervousness, the complete trust all had in their commander and his three senior NCOs and, as always, they plodded forwards as the screaming shells of their supporting barrage soared overhead and crunched ahead of them on the enemy lines. Up went the request for counter-battery fire – flares like huge bunches of flowers, slowly fading in brilliance as they fell to earth.

'In the centre of his platoon, your son walked at a sensible pace ahead of me as I did the usual infantry plod to his right. We had a steepish climb up to the enemy wire and when near the top, in the hellish bedlam of shell bursts – the ripping tracer from the German mg 34 machine gun. The noise, the dust, the mixed lights, flares, shells even searchlights giving the general axis of attack, the usual dry throat, sweat, stumbling, tripping, falling, forever seeking some form of cover when the enemy fire could be located and returned by the front Bren gunners for covering fire as the last assault was to be made.

'Although it was night, the darkness was constantly illuminated by shell bursts, flares etc. and a very pitiful-looking moon doing its best to penetrate the smoke and noise.

'We were close to the enemy gun pits when a sudden stab of light to our front seared through the darkness. It was, as I well knew, the first of several bursts of machine gunfire.

'Taking some form of cover was a first impulse and the platoon well spread out took what cover they could find. Our two Bren gunners were quickly in action but not quickly enough to deter the second burst of fire from the weapon. I saw Lieutenant Burns sag and fall to his knees as if in prayer and then fall sideways onto the ground. I called to Corporal Muir, "Take over" and hurried to aid Lieutenant Burns. He lay on his back, breathing in gasps – his helmet at the back of his head cupped almost like a pillow. I could see from ripped and torn pieces of his battledress that several bullets had penetrated his upper chest. As I placed my arm beneath his shoulders to place him in a more comfortable and if possible remedial position, I felt the blood seeping from the wounds. I had seen too many such wounds not to know their usual fatal results. His face was ashen, drained of the life I once knew so well as "my officer" and friend. He opened his eyes, gazed at me, recognised me, thank God, and said softly and quietly although obviously in great pain, "Take care of them, Sergeant MacDonald" and I said, "I'll do that, sir, you know" – "and yourself, Angus," were his last words to me as he died. No one was going to loot the body of "my lieutenant". I removed his Webley pistol and lanyard and stuffed them in my battledress blouse. I removed as gently as I could from his still-warm wrist the wristlet watch – to comply, if I lived, with his wishes. I grabbed a rifle and bayonet from Private Campbell who was carrying an extra one left by one of our walking wounded making his way back to a rear regimental aid post.

'I upturned the rifle and stuck its bayonet point in the ground close to the dead body – I took the steel helmet from beneath his head and hung it over the butt of the upended rifle to mark his location. As I did so, a small amount of blood seeped from within the helmet and ran slowly down the entire length of the rifle before dripping to the ground. It was as though it wanted to return to the body and make it warm and alive again.

'Task done, I told Private Campbell to run back to Company HQ and inform them of Burns' death and the marked location of his body, the watch I had removed I placed in my battledress blouse and amidst that hellish noise of battle, stood up, faced the body, stood to attention and saluted – and that's when the tears ran freely. With the back of my hand I swept them away. I turned to the scattered platoon and shouted, in an unbroken voice,

"Right, you lot, let's go and sort that shower out," – and we did just that – not without further casualties though, and unfortunately, I was one of them. A head wound sustained just outside Tunis causing distorted and partial vision and the reason I write this in large script as a patient in a military general hospital. Seemingly there is to be no more soldiering for me, but, I will become a VIP in my own right (a visually impaired person), but I'll remember those last words of "my brave and loyal lieutenant": "and youself, Angus," – I have but one Celestial Request to make, Special Friend, take care of Robert, there has never been since a Burns Night I have failed to attend and when that last song is sung I take that cup of kindness and know it will ever be filled "for the sake of Auld Lang Syne", on those occasions, I have linked hands with many but always wish that one of them was "my brave Lieutenant Robert Burns". This country may forget him, but we who are left to grow old, will still remember.'

FURTHER EVENTS

Wymms Farm
24 Cumbria Lane
Gt Cumbria
Ayrshire
Scotland
Tel: 07364 1582

Dear Sgt MacDonald,

Thank you so much for your kind letter regarding my son, Lieutenant Robert Burns. It meant so much to us as a family to have such news of his passing and your care for him on that tragic day.

I wonder if, and when, you are discharged from hospital (I do so hope it will not be a lengthy stay) you might find time to visit us at the address above.

My son told me in a letter home once that you lived in Largs which of course is just across the water from us. There would be no need to catch the ferry for I possess a small motor cruiser with, thank goodness, sufficient fuel in these tight days – and so could pick you up at the pier at a time and date suitable to you – tides permitting of course. But, if you telephone me beforehand, we could make mutual and suitable arrangements. If you might be able to stay awhile with us it would be a real pleasure to provide accommodation. Do please try to give this request and travel suggestions your blessing – it would mean so much to us to hear about our son and his life with you all – he called 'My platoon, the best, Dad,' as I am sure it was.

Thank you again, Sgt MacDonald, for your kindness in writing to us – I look forward to meeting you as 'a friend' just as Robert was to you.

Yours sincerely and gratefully,
Alistair Burns and family.

24 Royal Avenue
Largs
Ayrshire
Scotland
Tel: 0131 2322

Dear friend,

I hope not too informal a salutation, Mr Burns, but I was so pleased to receive your letter so used the informal 'friend'.

I have looked up the relevant tide times being a former boat owner myself, and I think there will be enough water at Largs pier at 0900 hrs on Saturday the date in question.

I would like to take up your offer of an overnight's stay so will bring a small case for the appropriate items, as we used to say in military school. Pinker brush and shaving stick – as laid out for kit inspections.

It is most kind of you to invite me and I shall endeavour to be an acceptable guest. My warmest regards to your family.

Your friend,
Angus MacDonald.

STILL FURTHER EVENTS

And so, the day dawned and at the hour stated, I clambered down to Alistair's boat after handing my small case down to him. Once aboard, he spun the vessel neatly astern and off we went. It was a fresh early summer morning, a modest swell, seagulls following us – expecting part of a catch. On our arrival at the island the tide was still making as Alistair nudged the boat alongside a small platform leading to his small boathouse. I had been to the island once or twice during my youth and remembered that this farmland led down to the shoreline. We moored and tied up neatly – and he approved my bowline mooring knots, and I think, from that moment, as two boatmen, we became true nautical friends as well.

A brief walk up to the farm and my case was taken from me by a really handsome woman he introduced as his wife, Christine. I was shown to a small bedroom, so obviously prepared for my stay – everything so clean and comfortable. The lace curtains billowed silently as an outside breeze caught them as I entered the room and rustled the stems of some early summer flowers in a vase on the dressing table. It was a room that almost spoke to me and said, 'Angus, old friend – this was my room and now it is yours.' Nonsense of course, but I was moved just by being there. I placed my few items where expected and went downstairs to the sitting room where they awaited me.

'All shipshape, Angus?' he asked.

'Fine, sir,' I replied and saw that another lady stood with him and his wife. I knew his son had once referred to his sister Margaret, when I had had occasion to collect the company mail, and handed several letters to him on my return. He was with another officer at the time and I heard him say, "Goodo – a letter from my sister."'

'Lucky you, Robert, remember me to her when you write.'

A further conversation between them ensued but I left to distribute the rest of the much awaited mail. But, I assumed, that his sister was a popular lady and well liked by at least one of his brother officers.

'And this is Margaret, my daughter, Angus, who has come home, especially to meet you.'

I believe we both extended our hands in greeting at the same time, we seemed to be so anxious to meet – she to see this Sgt MacDonald her brother had spoken about (so warmly, I hoped earnestly) and I to meet the sister of "my officer".

'May I call you Angus?' she said after our introduction.

'I'd consider it a pleasure,' I returned.

A small lunch had been prepared on a table in the large kitchen-cum-dining room. I saw the 'tattie scones' nestling on a plate and perhaps my eyes lingered on them sufficiently long enough to show my interest, for they were my favourite.

We sat four-square at the table, Margaret taking over the tea requirements from her mother, Christine. I needed no bidding from her father to 'tuck in, Angus', I did so and it was one of those small utterly delightful meals one remembers always – friendly undemanding conversation, all of us aware that a favourite son and brother was missing and I knew that later we would share his memory as a lasting bond between us.

I glanced occasionally rather than looked pointedly,

at each of my companions during the meal. The family closeness between them was very evident in every gesture, words said and unsaid, and strange to say, I felt they included me in that closeness.

As the bearer of good news, even though my mission was, in itself a sad one, to all their questions about their son and "his platoon" I knew I was able to give answers that they eagerly awaited and knew that they would be kind to his memory.

It is an odd thing to have a kind of sixth sense on occasion, and to know, as I did then, that Robert wherever he was, approved of my being there as a comforter and friend to his loved ones.

They made my brief stay overnight a pleasant one, chatting together of an evening with a wee dram or two shared with Alistair and then to bed – I ushered there by 'Goodnight and sleep well,' from them all.

I was tired but lay awake briefly recounting the day's events and the warmth of the friendship extended to me.

Alistair and I pushed the boat out literally on the following morning and a brief trip across the river to Largs, with a following tide took no time at all.

Alistair grasped my hand in parting and merely said, 'You now know where to find us, Angus – don't leave it too long before you come again, God bless you, lad.'

And so I returned to my lodgings in Royal Avenue, greeted my landlady Mrs Taylor, who mothered me as if I were her son – lost at sea during the war – she elicited news of my brief stay, made me a cup of her 'glorious tea', as she called it, brought it up to me in my room and went down to attend to other homely demands on her time from her other two tenants.

Alone in my room, I sipped the tea slowly, pleased that the customary two sugars had been observed – despite her 'Shouldn't you know – too much sugar is not good for you', but it was good for me then to muse over the events as I drank slowly and contentedly. I knew I had brought comfort to Alistair and his family, I know "my officer" approved of my aid to his loved ones. I knew also, that I wanted to be with them again – and, if it were possible – in the not too distant future. They were such nice, giving, kind people. Margaret had told me of her work as a medical secretary in a local hospital. Her two employers, both consultants, thought highly of her (as Alistair informed me) and why not, she was a truly beautiful young woman about my own age, thirtyish, I think. Her looks like those of "my officer" were unforgettable, fair wavy hair, blue eyes, and an easy grace. And so I mused on about my own affairs. My proposed activity as a visually impaired person – what could I do, with but a modest disablement pension, very little capital or collateral security as it was called by those in charge of disposable funds – obviously I had employment to seek and ran through the possibilities in my mind. Finding no immediate answers, I returned the teacup to glorious Mrs Taylor, extended profuse thanks to ensure a further cup of the nectar in the morning and went out for my gentle and careful constitutional.

It was still wartime, holidaymakers were few, various uniforms, and army, navy and air force were in evidence as I walked slowly along the seafront. I liked Largs, it was my birthplace and that of both my parents, who had died two years previously during an air raid on Glasgow when visiting friends. I was their only child, and bright enough but with only a modest educational background and my early occupations were such unlikely to lead to any appointments of value monetarily or significantly.

Thus, the army beckoned. Long before war came in 1939. As a Scot, I chose a Scottish regiment – the

Gordon Highlanders (although a wee bit of a Lowland Scot myself). I was fit and took to army life as a possible worthwhile career with my eyes, even for a youngster, firmly on educational improvement and then with appropriate qualifications make an attempt to get a commission – even a short-service one if need be.

I took to soldiering – took the requisite army certificates of education, served wherever sent, kept out of serious trouble, qualified in all small arms, and as a reward for these efforts was duly promoted, reaching in due course as would befit a regular soldier, the rank of sergeant. As such, certain military perks came my way, mess life, three chevrons on both upper sleeves and, a platoon of my own – well shared with a platoon officer – eventually Lt Robert Burns when going overseas to the Middle East. For many it was their first experience of battle, but I had served with the battalion in France in late 1939 early 1940 and was one of a few members of our division – the 51st Highland Division – to escape from St Valéry and get to a port where a navy ship rescued us and took us back to the UK.

Such was my brief history of conflict between us and the mighty German Army. On the ship taking us from Liverpool to Egypt via West and East Africa and the Red Sea and Suez Canal, Lt Robert Burns showed management skills not expected of one so young – he was twenty-one. I became his platoon sergeant and we would compare notes on each and every one of our fifty-man platoon – who would be qualified for what, riflemen, Bren gunners, stretcher-bearers, grenade throwers (for distance and accuracy). He was meticulous in his note taking – names, nicknames, proficiency awards, family and personal backgrounds, strengths and weaknesses, availability, smartness – he left nothing un-noted or to chance. 'Observation,' as he said to me once, when I was at Sandhurst, 'Sergeant MacDonald, I was told that if

I look after my men, they would look after me, and I believe I was told the truth.'

On my return to Royal Avenue, I found a letter addressed to me. It was unfamiliar handwriting and I was both surprised and happy to find it was from Margaret – thanking me for my visit and the pleasure it gave her and her parents to hear of the deeds and way of military life her adored brother had led. She expressed the hope that we might meet up, perhaps in a local restaurant or whatever place I considered suitable for her to hear more of the life her brother and I had led, at home and abroad. She included her phone number and explained that any evening call after 6 p.m. would find her. It was 'a few lines' as she wrote. Just in hope that the meeting could be to our mutual benefit. She would leave the matter to my discretion. Later the same evening I phoned and suggested arrangements that met with her instant approval.

I would have liked to have prolonged the call but made it a brief non-intrusive call as I was aware of her employment commitments as necessitating perhaps a late homecoming.

We met as arranged, on the afternoon of the following day at the entrance to one of the main restaurants in Largs. It was a fine sunny afternoon and she suggested we might walk for a while on the seafront. Eventually, we found an unoccupied bench and sat, and when seated, she asked me if her brother had been well looked after as he was such a young novice in matters of man management, especially in military matters. She looked at me so closely when posing this question – her voice gentle and enquiring, a kind of seeking solace for her loss.

'I understand your concern, Margaret, for at the time he took over the platoon, I was anxious that we would not lose him to another "Mob" as we called all the platoons etc., that might make a claim for him. He was instantly likeable, efficient, and knowledgeable on many things military, but looked so young and eager to do well. I suggested to him after our introduction by our company commander, that with his permission I would propose a Private Charles Campbell in our platoon, as his batman. His reply (a typical one I thought at the time) was:

Is he a good soldier, Sgt MacDonald?

One of the best, sir – cheerful, hardworking and well worth promoting to an NCO's rank, lieutenant corporal or corporal – but he prefers, as he calls it 'anonymity in the rank and file'. He actually used that word, Sergeant?

He did, sir – quite a bright lad – a good educational background, and although conscripted in his age group, he had the making of a fine soldier. He likes poetry, by the way, sir.

Does he indeed!

Yes, and writes a fair verse or two himself.

We have a prodigy in our midst, then, Sergeant! and I'd be most pleased if you would ask him, if he would take on that onerous military task.

I've already sounded him out on the posting, sir, and he agreed immediately, his words were, 'And when do I start, Sergeant?' He looked so keen and willing; I had to reply, 'Looks like you've already started, Campbell.' I'll send him along to your quarters if you are returning to them immediately?

Thank you, Sergeant MacDonald, I appreciate your concern and that affinity between you both!

'It was an enigmatic retort, but it took but a second on my part to fraternally join our two names, Campbell and MacDonald, without reference to Glencoe.'

'And they got on famously, did they, Angus? My brother and Campbell?'

'Yes, it was a most suitable choice, for Campbell was always cheerful and when I told your brother he was known in the platoon as "Cheerful Charlie Campbell", your brother said:

Alliteration at its best, Sergeant, I rather take to 'Charlie to the power of three'.

Meaning, sir?' I queried.

Or just C2 – I could knock one off and make it 'Charlie Squared'.

'He said it humorously to me but "CCC" he becomes known as then just "CC" and all knew who we referred to.'

'I often wondered about that reference to his batman in his letters – quite an apposite appellation – or is that a bit too posh, Angus?'

'No, Campbell was devoted to him, like all of us. We had the usual tough ones in our platoon, of course, all units have them, but even they made good under his influence and leadership.'

'And yours of course, Angus.'

'Well, that's kind of you to say so, Margaret, but I suppose I did help a bit along the way.'

'He spoke always so highly of you, his platoon Sergeant MacDonald. He called you a seasoned warrior, with your military medal and M.I.D. awarded in France in 1940.'

'Just deeds of daring, Margaret, some get them, some don't. I was lucky; an officer was nearby when I removed some blazing boxes of ammunition from a truck on fire as a result of a shell hitting it, not a large calibre one fortunately. Otherwise, it would have been "my hopping pot", as we soldiers said of one's demise.'

'I'm so pleased, Angus, to be able to trade these mutual remembrances of Robert. I miss him so very much and even though I was his elder sister by a few years, we had such fun together and he taught me how to play the piano, a good game of tennis and many other things.'

'And you, Margaret?'

'Oh, I taught him to dance – a prerequisite in the Highland Division so I am told – the GOC Tan Kimberley, liked his officers to display their reels etc.'

'Yes, we were all aware of that. But his dancing was ballroom-flavoured and I suppose infra dig.'

'I don't wish to boast, Angus, but I once won a gold medal in ballroom dancing!'

'Really, Margaret? I am really impressed – too crowded here for an exhibition of course?'

'Sadly so.'

'Well, perhaps one day a final waltz may be ours, or is that too premature a request?'

'We shall see, Angus, we shall no doubt see.'

We sauntered back to the restaurant and a pot of tea and a slice or two of my favourite Dundee cake (in wartime too!).

I was never a great one conversation-wise, but she was a good listener, and I honestly believe I excelled myself on that occasion.

Later I saw her off at the bus stop. She was returning to her small flat in Wymms Bay, a few miles further west along the coast.

As she boarded the bus, she turned and asked, 'Do I see you again, Angus?'

'I'd like that very much,' I replied.

'And soon?' she asked.

'Very soon, I'll phone if that's okay?'

'It is, Angus, goodbye.'

And for but a few days she stepped out of my life, but not and most certainly not, out of my thoughts before our next meeting. In that short space of time, I saw her in my mind almost everywhere. I'd pick up newspaper headlines, 'The Prime Minister said . . .' 'Margaret is beautiful' I would add; a book title *Sense and Sensibility* – 'and Margaret' I would add; salutations in the correspondence I had to always begin 'My Dear Margaret'. Even when I saw a picture of the King and Queen with their daughter, Margaret, I would visually substitute my own Margaret and think I must in future write to her as 'My Dear Princess'. It almost became an overwhelming feature in my daily life. Visionary expectations of life had done their best to rectify the abysmal gaps in my education – obtained a degree – eventually by a lengthy correspondence course, and hoped one day providing the vision held in my one reasonably good eye, would hold out until my possible retirement age. But always, in the back of my mind was to become part of a family again – I as an only son and the army had been my calling and my family. But a war and its human consequences had intervened. I had had one or two girlfriends, but they had married elsewhere – my uncertainty, mistrust of my abilities, always to blame for non-continuance of such brief affairs. A bit on the shy side where dalliances with the so well-named fair sex were concerned – but now, there was a titular change in my affairs of the heart. The letter M became prominent. My parents had been happily married but again, each was an only child, and age and time had whittled down possible relatives of a close kind. But, back again to Margaret – I knew so little about her personality that I was forever building up curricula vitae for her. Here it always began with ABC – Amazingly Beautiful Companion (or Charming in its adjectival use and rightly so!). Unmarried? Big query – does she want me? (I hope so, very earnestly I hope so); do I like her? What a silly question to ask, of course I do – I've fallen in love with her, it's obvious. And then I would stop the CV and get on with my work as an executive officer in the civil service. That would lead to my own assessment of myself:

Work prospects? Steady and reliably directed towards long useful service and a well-deserved and hard-earned pension (eventually!).

Physical attributes (if any)? Thirty-three years of age, a

true Scot, educated to a reasonable standard.

Experience of (a) life (b) love and war? Answers, (a) appropriate for age (b) limited. I'm sure others of use to append but what?

Can dance with both feet in unison and with the musical tempo allegro (but not fast).

Like children? Love them all to bits.

Aspirations? To be a good husband and father.

Anything else? Not at the moment but will give further thought to the matter.

But why stop at a CV for us both? Why not dream a little. One may lie in the gutter but still see the stars (I suppose the poet was writing at night?). So why not write to Margaret and express my true feelings, throw them on those fires of love and hear them sizzle with eagerness and ability to please.

To start, therefore:

My Dear Margaret (better delete possessive 'my' she is not mine yet?). No, it is simply not on – what a ridiculous supine way to conduct the overture to a proposed courtship. I'll phone instead. And I did, boldly and authoritatively I made the call. Dead on 6 a.m. the following day.

We marry, I assist her in running Wymms Farm – her parents watching us closely. We make the mistakes they, too, made when they were young farmers. It is always pleasant to come in from a day's work on the farm – hard agricultural and a sort of dairy farming – and see our young twin girls one each to a grandparent sitting between them – no doubt enlightening them on the day's schooling. We look at each other, Alistair and Christine, and no words need be said but he always says them.

In a pram nearby sleeps our son, and as always Alistair looks at us both, nods towards the pram and says, 'A bonny wee lad, Angus.'

And my reply also, is always the same 'Aye, Robert is just that.'

Then he says, 'One would have to go a thousand miles to find another like him.'

'Or even higher perhaps, Alistair?'

As always, he takes my point – looks at the evening clouds building up tinged with just a Speck of Dusk, 'Aye,' he says for he knows as I do that with our mutual memories we are never alone – there is present that absent friend.

And Margaret too knows, and kisses her father, the twins, but always the baby first. I receive my one, as she smiling says when I ask, 'In due course . . . my bonny lad.' And these due courses are many as she says, 'You deserve them, my dear Angus MacDonald, former bachelor of this parish.'

I never finished that CV of hers, maybe one day I shall make a kite of the papers and as it sails higher and higher I'd like to hope "my officer" and his Special Friend will ring their benediction back to earth – but a flight of fancy of course – but one never knows? For not all of us live lives of quiet desperation – for we have youngsters to care for and the future of my beloved Scotland lies with them. I must be one of the meek ones for I have inherited at least a part of the earth. And my kite? It is not finished yet but one day my children may fly it – and I and "my officer" will be there to push it gently back to earth, to the safe hands of our children.

CHAPTER 7

LAMAL

'Good afternoon, Easton. May I join you on your constitutional?'

'Please do, H.C. I was musing on the way Holmes and his nurse get along so well together.'

'Oh, you too, Easton, have noticed it? That readily betokens a qualification surely? Perhaps an explanation would be more acceptable to you?'

'I see mystery upon mystery is to become the conversational subject today, H.C.?'

'Yes, it is a pleasant little tale and I think that the fertile mind of Holmes will eventually put all the facts together and write his own story concerning the Celestial Request we received a long time ago. Come, let us sit comfortably on this my favourite bench, and I shall do my best to enlighten you.'

'The Request came from a young Indian girl named Lamal; a lovely name, I think, Easton?'

'Yes, it is Hindustani for the word jewel.'

'Knowledgeable you, Easton, with your Hindi picked up on your travels – but to continue. She asked if I, as her Special Friend, could pass on her grateful thanks to a very kind man whose name she did not know who had sent money to a charity by the name of Smile Train. Apparently a group of doctors, surgeons and nurses, and all their equipment, travelled from England to India where their skills repaired the unsightly damage caused by cleft palates, lips etc., on young children born with these physical defects. She, Lamal, was one of those with a cleft palate, causing her much distress at school and limited what little social activity was available to her. Her operation was a great success and when she asked the surgeon the name of the person who had sent the money to help her, he said, 'I personally don't know who this person is, young lady, but charity is so often sweeter when it is silent.'

'She had always remembered this remark and since I was a kind man, I would know who her benefactor is and could I pass on her heartfelt thanks.

'She said that a small note accompanied the donation, and it merely said *With love and good wishes to a young Indian girl whose name I do not know – hoping that this small gift will bring you much happiness. From someone who cares.*

'She knew, she said, that I was a busy person, but would I fit it in her Request if I could find a little space for it, when I could find time to do it?

'So, to return to Lamal – she grew up to be a beautiful young woman. Her mother was a member of a good family and her father was a minor civil servant in a government department in Delhi. The family circumstances did not permit of immediate surgical treatment to Lamal's condition. It was difficult for her at school and to make close friends, but she coped to the best of her abilities. Her kind and cheerful disposition drew the attention of a doctor who had connections with a charity in England where surgeons specialised in the treatment of facial disfigurement etc. It was a charity supported by donations from well-disposed and kind-hearted persons, always willing to help others, particularly children.

'A leaflet showing photos of the children needing help

was sent out to donors specifying an amount of money necessary for each operation. The donor in Lamal's case did not specify a particular child as depicted in the leaflet, but left it to those involved to find a child in need. He also wished to remain, as he stated, 'A person who cares'. It was this fact that formed the subject of her Request.'

'An interesting story so far, H.C. – sorry I interrupted you – do please continue, for I believe I have established in my mind the connection between Lamal and her present name, Constance Dickens.'

'You are correct, Easton, but shall we go in? The sun is setting.'

'Not just yet, please, H.C. Explain the reason for the change of name from Lamal to her present name.'

'Well, the change was effected legally by deed poll sometime later in her life when, as a qualified nurse, a vocation she chose as her calling, she was engaged by a wealthy elderly lady in England.

'For several years she was nurse/carer and close companion to her employer who had been a widow for several years, and years previously had lost her only daughter, named Constance, in a fatal traffic accident. It had occurred one foggy November night on a motorway when the vehicle in which she was a passenger was involved in a multi-vehicle collision. There were several fatalities, of whom her young daughter was one.

'Lamal's loyalty, efficiency and cheerfulness greatly impressed her employer, a Mrs Christine Dickens, who one day asked Lamal if she had a family and siblings. On being told that Lamal was an only child and that her parents had been killed in a severe earthquake in India, she asked Lamal if she would like to change her name by deed poll to Constance Dickens. Lamal had no objection to this suggestion, but insisted that Lamal should remain part of her new name. Eventually, as always happens, Easton, both parties came to us and that is where the story ends.

Lamal's arrival was premature caused by her contracting a fever of unknown origin, as it is called in medical terms. She was at my request, chosen to be the carer/nurse of Holmes and a splendid job she had made of it. I believe that she is now by name a member of a distinguished literary family since her employer was related to that splendid author of the Victorian era.

'What a feather in his cap for Holmes to have such a helper in all his literary endeavours, and searches in the archives.

'And, Easton, there is yet to be a denouement in this story. For one day Lamal will discover that Holmes was the 'kind man' to whom her thanks were to be given.'

'Or even perhaps, H.C., Holmes will discover his generosity as a donor to Smile Train brought such a wonderful person into his life and made it even more worthwhile. I'm sure he is bound to make a story of it.'

'What title do you think it might have, Easton?'

'"Great Revelations", possibly? And he'll claim the resulting story came up to their mutual great expectations.'

'Quite so, Easton, especially if it has co-authors, titles Holmes and Dickens – until tomorrow?'

'Until then, H.C. I'm sure that punctual sun will be out to greet us then.'

'Yes, Easton, as C. J. H. Dickens once wrote in his *Pickwick Papers*, the sun is a punctual servant of all those who work and we most certainly do that here on Nimbus 9. All in a good cause though – simply a labour of love on behalf of that Speck of Dust, Holmes has taken to his heart.'

CHAPTER 8

SEMPER FIDELIS

'Hello – Easton! Just the person I wanted to see! Do please join me in this wonderful afternoon sunshine; room enough, as always, on this bench of mine.'

'I think we all know this is your favourite spot, H.C.,' replied his companion, doing as bidden.

'I've been thinking,' continued H.C. 'that the short story we put together on your Request, did not run out too badly. Might it be possible, do you think, for yet another joint effort in regard to a Request, made again a long time ago, by Holmes himself?'

'Yes, I'm sure it would be, H.C. After all, we have the Requests of me, Connie Lamal Dickens, Ludovic Kaye, and others put into story form – so why not a story on the great storyteller himself?'

'Knowing Holmes though, Easton, he'd brighten it up a little if he knew.'

'True, H.C., but it is simply a résumé of the work he has undertaken on behalf of so many others and perhaps, a raison d'être might emerge for some of those strong anti-war views he holds so dearly?'

'Yes, Easton, a good reason why we should not delay in our task. It started long ago when as a young Irish lad, he lost his grandparents during the difficult potato famine in Ireland. They were terrible, terrible times, with so much suffering and eventual hatred of the authorities who failed in many ways to rectify the situation. Ireland, as you know yourself, Easton, is a wonderful land, and not called the Emerald Isle for nothing. They are a gifted race, in many things; music, art, literature, dances, engineering, strongly religious in many quarters. There's Celtic blood there sufficient for two Irelands – a sad political history also with sectarianism and warring factions. Holmes, as a young boy, adopted by an aunt when his parents died, was brought up in this disturbed atmosphere and loathed the conflict.

'He was an intelligent, bright young lad, quite good-looking in that Irish masculine way, did well in his studies at school, took up playing the violin and played it like an angel (as his aunt once told him – it pleased him no end, for he liked the word angel and has done so ever since).

'During that horrible, senseless war of 1914–1918, like many young Irish lads, he joined the army and served, at first as a young infantryman in the 36th Irish Brigade in Belgium and northern France. He saw some terrible sights and his experiences in that war taught him in no uncertain manner, to hate, loathe and abhor (his words) from the bottom of his very heart, war and aggression of any kind. Later in the war he was one of the British troops sent to Italy to support the Italian Army high up in the Alpine region fighting the Austro-German forces. He liked the Italians and became a close friend of an Italian liaison officer attached to his battalion. At the time, 1917–1918, he had been commissioned in the field for some deeds of exceptional bravery, and was a full lieutenant. It was difficult campaigning country – rock-hard mountainous surfaces, ice, snow, rivers in spate – dreadfully difficult to survive in physically without the appendages of war, artillery, gunfire from various weapons, and splintering of rock faces when hit by shells, sharp, hot pieces of metal and rock scattering in all directions. He and his Italian friend, a Captain Antonio Verde, became close friends and, on one short leave, out of the line, he was invited by Antonio to stay with him and his family in a small village in San Lorenzo.

'Here, Holmes met the sister, Angelina, of his friend and was, as he said, absolutely smitten, bowled over, instantly in love. Although the family were bilingual in Italian and English, he put himself out to master as much of their language as possible. I think the Irish have that musical way of speaking that tends to lend itself to both French and Italian. I think also, that there is a strong family closeness and love that forms a bond of a kind. Holmes did well in his linguistic attempts and he and Angelina become close friends. They wrote to each other, he in his best Italian, and she in her best English and were teachers to each other in such a loving and friendly way.

'The bitter winter fighting went on and, one day during a severe artillery bombardment, he was with his friend, Antonio, when a huge jagged piece of an explosive shell inflicted a terrible, mortal wound on his companion. The shrapnel had severed Antonio in two from the waist down. He, Holmes, had never been able to come to terms with that terrible wound and the few seconds after it occurred, he heard his former wonderful companion cry out in pain for his God's aid. Antonio was beyond all human aid and so, for a long time afterwards, was Holmes. The tragic loss of his friend, and the family back in San Lorenzo during an air raid by enemy bombers caused a kind of a mental and physical indifference to everything about him.

'Utterly indifferent to danger, he led dangerous patrols, did extra covering duties for brother officers, who were close to the end of their endurance. He never took another leave out of the line – his conduct ensured promotion to captain and he took every opportunity to enhance his mastery of the Italian language (when asked about this he said it was a devotional duty in memory of two wonderful Italian friends). He committed several Italian songs to memory and sang them (so I am told) with a wonderful Irish lilt.

'The war ended and the passing he had envisaged for himself and tried very hard to bring about did not occur. And, Easton, that was the Request he made: why, what he sought, did not happen and why were his friends taken from him? And as a survivor, what was he wanted for when so many others who had harmed no one, were taken away?'

'I think I know the answer to that Request, H.C.'

'Yes, it is obvious to us both – but not to himself. He was told that there is a reason for everything happening on earth and in the lives of people everywhere. He was told that as a result of a kind act, he would shortly make, all would be made known to him.'

'And it obviously occurred, H.C.'

'Yes, he was serving still in the army and when out driving on some military enquiry, was held up by a military policeman halting traffic to enable a cable to be affixed to a strong tree growing by the road edge which abutted in a steep incline of fifty yards a lake in which an army mobile crane had gone off the road and fallen into the edge of the lake in about six feet in depth of water. The vehicle had fallen on its wheelbase at an angle where the driver could still be seen in the vehicle's cab. The weight of the vehicle was tilted waterside and a cable attached to a strong section of it and efforts were being made to winch the vehicle upright and if possible, out on the bank of the lake. It appeared that the driver had been knocked unconscious as a result of the fall and that the water level was gradually rising to flood the cab. Holmes left his vehicle, hurried to the front of a small row of parked vehicles, ascertained very quickly what was happening and clambered down the bank, removed his shoes and jacket and plunged in to aid the driver. His actions were so swift and urgent that he ignored, or possibly didn't hear, the warnings of those trying to effect the recovery of the vehicle and to save its driver from drowning, that it was a dangerous undertaking and there was a possibility that the one wire cable used was not strong enough for the job. Therefore, the work was to keep the vehicle held in the position it had until further mechanical help of a stronger nature arrived. Holmes though, could see that long before such help arrived and the approach road cleared of traffic and observers of the incident, the vehicle would slip further away into deeper water.

'His knowledge of such military vehicles told him the cab door would be unlocked and before it submerged and made opening the cab door against the pressure of the water therefore difficult, an attempt at this moment to get to the cab and getting the unconscious driver out was a possibility not to be missed. Holmes was last seen clambering up to the cab with one hand on the door handle when the cable snapped and both free ends viciously whipped and lashed around anything in their path, before their momentum ceased. The cable end attached to the vehicle spun back and knocked an unconscious Holmes into the water just as the vehicle now unchecked, slid deeper into the lake surface. Holmes was drowned and came to us here at Nimbus 9, where he met the driver who was already dead in his cab before Holmes made the effort to save him.'

'No wonder he is so well liked here in Nimbus 9 and elsewhere on his travels. And was he ever told of his eventual carer/nurse here, H.C.?'

'Not in so many words – it was left to his undoubted investigational skills to find the answer for himself.

Holmes has always helped others, and I think was aware of that phrase "Greater love hath no man . . ." etc., etc., when he was but a child.'

'And he seems to be an exception to that saying, which includes the words "When I was a child, I thought as a child, but when I became a man, I put away those childish things."'

'Yes, Easton, we are lucky to have Holmes in our midst, he serves us all well.'

'Yes, literally a case of *servitor servientum* – a servant of those who serve, I believe is the translation.'

'It is indeed, Easton, the words good and faithful are merited in his case also.'

'*Semper fidelis* of course.'

'Enough of the Latin tags, Easton! Now about this story – is it to be continued, or is this one example enough to cover a lifetime of such selfless acts on his part?'

CHAPTER 9

IT'S NOT ONLY IN THE MIND

'As you know, Easton, we celestes in our various grades, receive countless Requests and efforts are made by our many helpers to provide satisfactory answers to the problems that abound on that Speck of Dust. One, personally referred to me was from a small boy, very intelligent and a member of kind, loving parents, who wanted to know who God was and who made Him or Her? The boy said that his mother, when they went to church on a Sunday, had told him that he had to be on his best behaviour as he was in God's house. When they left, after the service, he asked his mother where God cooked in His house as he (the little boy) looked everywhere and could not see a kitchen or a stove or anything – only a place where God washed His hands before meals, so there had to be a cooking place somewhere with pots and pans, like at home.

'The mother was unable to give him a satisfactory answer and his father was away at sea, so he could not ask him, so he made the Celestial Request we are speaking about.'

'A very original Request from a small boy and was he provided with a satisfactory answer, H.C.?'

'Yes, Easton, I suppose that question has occupied the minds of many people – all seeking an answer. But, I remember a conversation long ago with Holmes who thought that in the Beautiful Beginning (he never refers to it as the Big Bang, such a noisy appellation, I think) the clouds of infinite species of dust from billions of galaxies, gathered together. Then, when the infinite scents, colours, tastes etc., had been apportioned to each gathering, grouping of galaxies occurred. These were given an abbreviated code identification name G.O.D. It became in constant use and the full stops were eventually omitted, thus being known simply as God (short for Galaxies of Dust). Ingenious thinker that Holmes, don't you think, Easton?'

'Decidedly so, H.C. He provided a name and its creator – this was passed to the young boy, H.C., I presume?'

'Yes, but not immediately as he spent several of his growing into manhood years trying to find an answer for himself.'

'Did he do so?'

'Yes, Easton, he was extremely happily married, had a family and thought such was a Celestial Gift/Answer to his boyhood Request. Then he lost his beloved father, then later his mother, and finally his beautiful loving wife who was once a supremely gifted ballet dancer. Those terrible losses were difficult for him to bear and he lost also faith and hope.'

'He regained it surely, H.C.?'

'But of course, Easton, he is now curator of our Archives Branch, specially chosen for the appointment.'

'No wonder he and Holmes and Nurse Dickens get along so well together – they each have an enquiring mind.'

'And don't forget, Easton, each has a warm and loving heart – essential prerequisites in their respective calling, don't you think?'

'Absolutely – "to the manor born", as it is said on that Speck of Dust. And I often wondered why Holmes referred to the curator as Ludo. Now I know, it is short for Ludovic. Well, well, no wonder they are an illustrious band, for Ludovic is a fine writer himself.'

'Yes, quite true, Easton. The title of his last book was *It's Not Only in the Mind*, after all. Shall I see you this evening?'

'But of course, H.C. I enjoy our chats; they seem always to lead to stories delivered by Holmes in his inimitable way!'

CHAPTER 10

THE SUMMER'S GONE

'Well, Easton, hope springs eternal, so I believe is often said. And we, on Nimbus 9 know all too well where that hope resides, do we not?'

'We do, indeed, H.C.'

'Do you remember, Easton, your own Celestial Request all those years ago?'

'I've never forgotten it, H.C. And once wrote a short story about it – no doubt Holmes would develop it in his inimitable style, but at least it is readable and makes so much sense to me, knowing now the reason for the aid and advice you gave.'

'Well, let us both reminisce together and see how our mutual story might compare with that by Holmes. Do you agree?'

'Yes, H.C. Your usual opening of course?'

'Naturally, Easton, they have, I think that homely touch. It will need a title, so thinking caps on.'

'I had given it "The Summer's Gone", H.C., but I believe I took that from "The Londonderry Air" – a tune I loved to play on my flute in days long ago.'

'Then, Easton, let it be used again. It is, after all, a season that comes again after each spring's rebirth, so let "The Summer's Gone" open in our usual way.

'As you know, Easton, my many assistants register

the huge number of Requests received and, in some cases, suggest a suitable answer to particular sets of circumstances.

'One such was in respect of a young soldier, severely injured in a traffic accident involving a military vehicle in which he was a passenger. It occurred at the end of that recent war during which he had married a very young country girl. They had been together for but a short time but it was a blissfully happy marriage. His injuries were such that he knew there was no hope for him, and he requested that "his angel wife" should not be left alone after his death, and that another soldier be found to comfort her in her grief and take good care of her until the time they could be together again. Such a simple, loving Request caused me to select such a young soldier, and during the war still going on, arranging for him to survive several bitter battles in the desert in which he was involved. He was then twenty-one years of age, had had a somewhat unsettled childhood – parents divorced, parted from his brothers and sister, the usual emotionally disturbed background that often sends the survivor in search of settled family contentment. Many of them tend to make several errors in their search, but it never deters them. Their persistence and determination is sometimes remarkable to behold and merits celestial assistance, such as you received, Easton, for you were the young soldier selected for me to safeguard and ensure you survived those two wounds you received.'

'Yes, H.C., an inch or two either way on each occasion and no more soldiering for me, would have been the result. I had seen so many of my comrades killed and wounded, and at the end of the war I felt that I had lost so many good friends, that I wondered why I was a survivor. I suppose many thought that way.'

'And do you remember your Request, Easton, when, in the summer of 1946, you were granted home leave for twenty-eight days after being absent from home for four years?'

'Yes, H.C., at the time it seemed an odd Request to make, but somehow I knew I was advised to make it.'

'It was good advice too, Easton, for we sent it before we had arranged for it to be met. You could continue this story from now on, Easton, if you wish?'

'Yes, my Request was that one day I might meet a young lady who needed a chap like me in her life to make up for disappointments etc. I felt I could bring happiness once again into life, that I was ever intended to find this love I had never known in my life. I had not found it on my own account – a bit too diffident, shy, backward in coming forward in such romantic incidents. Too uncertain for myself, I suppose, and so requested a spot of help. An odd sort of Request, I thought at the time and wondered if it might be answered.

'I was stationed in the occupation army in Austria at the time. I had about eighteen months left to serve of my regular army engagement of seven years with the Colours, as it was said in those days. I was a sergeant in a special investigation section – a reasonable investigator with quite a lot of experience in criminal and security matters, and pondering on whether to extend my military service for twenty-two years and make army life my career.

'But, in July 1946, I was granted twenty-eight days' leave, travelled by military transport to Harwich and then to London by train. Rail networks abroad were well and truly destroyed in those days hence the military transport. To digress a little, H.C., as a boy in a military school band I had been taught to play the flute. I had no opportunity during the war years to purchase one, until I arrived in London, and there, in a window of a pawnshop close to the railway station, I saw one for sale.

'The price was reasonable, and I bought it on sight. It was a truly beautiful instrument destined, I thought at the time, to belong to me. I then caught a Green Line bus and travelled to a small village, named Crays Hill, in Essex, where I had decided to spend my leave in a small one-bedroom cottage, owned by a friend of my mother. The property was in the centre of a small row of similar cottages, each detached with small gardens front and rear, and small low hedgerows dividing them.

'It was a pleasant summer, and I cooked my meals on a small stove, went to the local public house for refreshments and returned to my cottage; sat beneath an apple tree in the rear garden and played my flute, a bit rusty to start with, a soft tonal quality not to inconvenience the neighbours on either side, and felt quite at home in that small village. One afternoon when so engaged musically beneath my tree, a young girl from an adjoining cottage called to me, "Would you like a cup of tea, soldier?" for I was wearing army uniform at the time. I agreed at once that I would appreciate such a gift and she hurried back to the kitchen of her cottage and brought out the offered gift on a small tray and delicately passed it to me over the top of the hedge. She gave me a shy smile and returned to the kitchen that opened to the rear garden.

'I heard a woman's voice say, "And did he accept it?" and the reply was "Yes. I'm glad you told me to ask him, he seems a nice young man." And then the door closed and I heard no more remarks of appraisal concerning myself. When I returned the crockery etc., I met the sister, Iris, and husband, Fred, and the young girl who was introduced to me as Nonnie (not her real name, but one she had chosen for herself when a small child singing a song "Hey Nonnie No"). She was small of build, had a soft country tan, wide blue eyes and such wonderful friendly features. She was twenty-three years of age and her sister a few years older. The husband, Fred, about the same age as his wife, had been a former soldier in the Royal Army Medical Corps in the recent war. They had a small son, Michael, about four years of age and it was a close family, unlike my own. I was pleased to become a part of it. I learnt from Fred that Nonnie had been widowed about two years previous when her young husband had been killed in a tragic accident, that she often babysat for them and did not have much of a social life. She had a black springer spaniel named Prince and was greatly attached to him. "She had been hurt, Charles," he said, and then added, "so be kind to her."

'I had already made up my mind that was what I intended to do, once I could get to know Nonnie. And that was soon solved, for when I was about to return to my cottage, Nonnie asked me if I would like to go with her to pick mushrooms early next morning. Of course I agreed and at the appointed time, 6 a.m., I was ready at the gate, took one of the two baskets she carried from her and off we set for some lush meadows not too far away. A few cows, munching far from quietly, gave us a disapproving look, but did not interfere with our mushroom location tasks. When both baskets were almost full I suggested to her that we should each try to get a big mushroom and the winner of the biggest one would get a prize.

'It was a glorious morning in early August – a morning of a day I shall never forget. I won the competition, but only just and she asked me what prize I would like. I cannot in all truth say that I was very good in these romantic situations. Never having had much experience of them, but I asked for a kiss. We were sitting side by side on the grass at the time, and she leant across to me, closed her eyes, lifted her lips to mine and we kissed and I can't say we fell in love at that moment, for I had loved her from the time our hands had met on the tea tray – and that was but yesterday.

'We lay on our backs side by side on the softest of grasses – it surely must have been a heavenly meadow, her fingers twining in mine. Looking up at the blue sky as the day fully dawned. I turned my face to her and said, "I love you, Nonnie," and her reply was "I know."

'We returned to the cottage – made gifts of those mushrooms to neighbours and, after obtaining a licence, we married in the Brentwood Registry Office. The next day was the final day of my leave and I left that most wonderful country girl wife of mine with her sister in that wonderful little Essex village, and returned to my unit in Austria.

'Towards the end of the year, she joined me in married quarters in Velden, on the edge of the Worthersee, in Carinthia, Austria.

'For the next year or so we lived together in blissful happiness – I worked hard at my job as an investigator, was duly promoted and it seemed that a new life had begun for both of us.

'I intended to leave the army on completion of my service in 1948 and Nonnie and I would, with our savings, purchase a small cottage in the village. Alas, it was not to be. Nonnie began to have headaches that increased in severity, and began to tire easily and eventually in late 1948 we both returned to stay with her mother and stepfather in their house in the village. I obtained employment with Fred at a manufacturing firm locally – it was not too far or distant and we were able to cycle there and back each day. Nonnie, ever so brave and cheerful, slowly became pale and suffered terrible headaches and was in great pain. I summoned the local doctor one night and she was admitted to the general hospital in Southend, Essex. I visited her daily, taking a picture of the small local cottage we intended to purchase, and talked when she was able, through her bruised ulcerated lips. She was the most beautiful, the most wonderful girl I had ever known. Her unselfish love for me I know I did not really deserve. Although I did not quite know it at the time – she was my angel on earth.

'The doctors told me that the acute myeloid leukaemia she suffered from had no cure.

'Against their advice, I went to Harley Street and paid 100 guineas to a doctor who claimed to have a possible cure. It involved transfusions of blood through her body. I was told it was hopeless, but I was quite distraught and would do anything to save her. The so-called relief only caused her more pain (God forgive my stupidity).

'I next went to a Cancer Research establishment in London and offered myself as a guinea pig to enable some form of a cure to be found. The elderly doctor I saw, as we parted said, "It is not possible, my son, were it to be so, don't you think I might have thought as you do now?" I left, he stood at the doorway and shook my hand and wished me every success in my efforts.

'I did not return to my employment but spent as much time as I could at the hospital. I had seen death in the long war years behind me. I was called to the hospital one afternoon and was told she had died a little earlier in the day. I sat by her bedside, kissed the now pain-free lips and my tears fell upon her closed eyes.

'I looked at the ceiling, the walls and outside through the window at an uncaring world – or so I thought. It is so difficult (now and was then also) to understand why a piece of heaven, in an earthly angel being entrusted to one to take care of, to love intensely to the point of willing to give your life for her, and to wonder why it was to be taken away from me. She harmed no one, helped others (sent me out in the snow one Christmas time in Velden to bring in to our table, a poor ragged tramp-like figure she had seen through our window overlooking the street). I did her bidding and a very happy well-fed refugee possibly, left our small flat with all the small gifts he could carry, mostly foodstuffs of course.

'Oh, my lovely, beautiful, kindly, selfless country girl wife of so little a period of time. I weep still for you and I am no longer your young soldier promised to you by H.C. so long, long ago.

'In my mistaken belief that I could help her, I merely prolonged her agony. How stupid I was at that time – and how fatuous my blind unforgiveable endeavours.'

'No, Easton, you did what at the time you thought was right and it clouded every other thought. It is not at all easy to be wise before an event – hindsight comes later and becomes experience of life itself. It is said that one's fate is settled at one's birth – but Nimbus 9 does not hold with this belief – for so often people make purposeful decisions of their own and fate is not part of such actions that follow.

'You, Easton, know the gift given to you for that brief time all those years ago. You did your best to honour that trust – but, like so many others, you thought you had failed in some way or another. To err, Easton, is human, to forgive, divine.'

'Yes, H.C., how right you are. The world outside had its own individual problems – many people living lives of quiet desperation, and doing their best to cope day by day. But I did think my world had gone that sorrowful September day and longed to be with Nonnie in that peaceful, pain-free place. I don't think I actually put that wish into effect, but I did re-enlist in the army for the completion of my pensionable service, and in the next fourteen years served wherever I was sent. Did two three-year tours of service in Malaya/Singapore/Hong Kong etc. The Korean War was on but I remained in Hong Kong and Malaya at the time. Promotions came my way, commendations for investigations and enquiries well done and studied hard for a couple of degrees.'

'Law and the humanities, were they not, Easton?'

'Yes, H.C., but I was no Tommy Traddles who made a success of his calling, but more like his friend David Trotwood – alias Copperfield. I found I was not cut out for "Wig and Gown", not an analytical brain, I guess, or an undisciplined mind – even both.'

'Come now, Easton, you were an excellent investigator,

and that is why you were chosen to replace Holmes and, I might add, have done excellently. But the Guardian Angel Enquiry Branch was the appointment for you; we always had in mind, why your predecessor became the assistant curator.'

'And a fine job he is making of it, H.C., as Holmes will attest – Charles Doyle and Holmes get along famously.'

'Yes, Easton, their names have that easy on the ear correlation.'

'So they do, H.C. I hadn't thought of that.'

'And you a humanities man? Shame, Easton – until the next time?'

'Yes, H.C., a small brief to read from and I'll be there.'

'And, Easton, you sought that love over and over again – marital mishaps you lightly called them, but they were far from being that. They were part of the life you were destined to lead before being chosen to be a minister for the G.A. Branch at Nimbus 9. It is not only little children who had suffered to come unto us. There are many others you know.'

'Yes, H.C., many now know they have been given true, unselfish love, and when they lose it they consider their world is shattered. But I, H.C., lost my world itself. There was nothing left to shatter.'

'Ah, Easton – but you gained another with us all at Nimbus 9, now no more stories, we'll leave them to Holmes and his carer/secretary. I wonder when his archive searching will reveal to him the coincidental arrangements made for himself and his carer to meet.'

'That should be interesting, H.C.'

'Yes, we'll just have to be patient – until tomorrow, Easton?'

'But of course, H.C.'

'By the way, Easton, it was not an uncaring world, but only at that time an unknowing one.'

CHAPTER 11

COMPLEMENTARY GESTURES

'Hello, Easton! "Well met by midday" as a title of a story by Holmes would put it.'

'Good day to you, H.C. I was thinking of our conversation recently about that moving song "Old Man River" composed, lyrics and music, in your honour, I believe.'

'Yes, a favourite of mine – I try always to deserve that musical honorarium.'

'Over and over again you do, H.C., and that's no disguised flattery.'

'Talking of which, Easton, do you recall that commendation you received long ago and regarding an enquiry you were given to trace a missing three-year-old boy. It was well deserved and I'm sure Holmes would do full justice to "the facts of the case", as he calls them in his story-writing moments. Why not get both of your heads together (literally, of course) "and see what transpires", another term Holmes is fond of using.'

'Yes, I agree – we shall start at once on the project (if not sooner), as Holmes is bound to add. I'll bring the finished article along on my next visit.'

'Yes, Easton, please do. Until then, "bated breath" the order of the day?'

'Scarcely that, H.C. – it's just a simple tale of

coincidences – of which you are a master.'

'We had best stop these *honoris causa* to each other – until tomorrow then?'

'My pleasure, H.C.'

And so, as the saying goes (and often used by Holmes) "two heads being better than one" – the story was written as follows:

Charles Easton winced as the bullet struck his left shoulder and, at a slower pace than on entry, pursued its slow path across the top of his left shoulder to lodge quietly and, he thought, safely in his right shoulder, just below the surface of the skin.

Five months previously, he had been hit by shrapnel in the back, and he thought such injuries were perhaps justified by the fact as a machine gunner he had been actively engaged in causing such to the enemy. But no more time for such philosophic thoughts, it was necessary to hand over the machine gun to his number two, alongside him, busily feeding in another belt of ammunition to replace that just expended.

It was not a severe wound, a bit painful, entry wound bleeding a little, but nothing to prevent him from being 'walking wounded' once again as he trudged back to the regimental aid post and then on to a casualty clearing station. Here, away from the immediate clamour of the battlefield, he was seated on a chair, his bloodstained battledress blouse and shirt removed and given a cup of tea – 'You lot have earned it,' said the medical orderly, and added, proffering the mug of tea, 'the MO will see you in a moment – we are rather busy as you can see.'

Easton looked around in the tent and saw several severely wounded soldiers (some German and Italian) lying on stretchers. They were quiet and still and had obviously received some pain relief before further attention.

Easton felt a bit of a fraud with his slight wound – but it was speedily dealt with without the need of a local anaesthetic, by a young medical officer who neatly lanced the skin, removed the bullet with a pair of tweezers and then said, 'Do you want it as a souvenir?'

Easton accepted the offer; put it in the pocket of his blouse, and was sent onwards to a base hospital near Tripoli. Before leaving he thanked the doctor, who was about twenty-six years of age – about four years older than himself – for his prompt and efficient services, and promised not to make a habit of incurring such wounds. The doctor replied that as the entry and exit wounds were small, no sutures were required – but since gangrene might affect desert-acquired wounds, a short stay in hospital might be required for the wounds to heal. Easton did notice at the time that he experienced difficulty in lifting his arms but attributed this inability to initial shock to the muscles through which the round had travelled. As he went to find his small pack, the doctor picked it up for him and placed it in the rear of an ambulance which, with other stretcher cases, Easton boarded. Thanking him for his kindness, Easton jokingly said, 'If I can do a similar favour for you one day, sir, just ask.'

'Off you go, lad,' said the medical officer and closed the rear door of the ambulance.

Some nine years later, when Easton, now a sergeant in an army Special Investigation Branch unit based in Bras Basah Road, Singapore, was given the task of looking for a small boy missing from outside the married quarters of his parents, a Major Giles and his pregnant wife, Mrs Ann Giles. The officer concerned was a member of the Royal Army Medical Corps, based at Alexander General Hospital, near Gillmen Barracks, Singapore.

Easton drove to the venue as quickly as possible in his jeep, met the very distressed mother of the missing boy – obtained details of clothing worn, features etc., and examined the edge of a deep monsoon drain in the vicinity of the quarters. On the edge of the concrete drain, some six feet deep with tapered sides, he found partly wedged in its side, a small model car that the boy had obviously been playing with. He made immediate enquiries in the vicinity, producing a photograph of the young boy, but without a successful result. It was towards the end of the monsoon season and sudden rainfall had occurred a few hours before. He learnt that the father, Major Giles, was on his way back to his quarters, having been delayed in an urgent operation. But, it appeared from all the meagre evidence obtained, that the boy had accidentally fallen into the monsoon drain, at the base of which water ran into an adjoining river about ten feet wide. It appeared as if the boy had attempted to loosen his toy car, had lost his balance, fallen into the drain and was carried away in the somewhat dirty river itself. Since the depth of the water was about three to four feet – he removed items from his trouser pockets, vehicle keys etc., and placed them in the upper pockets of his tunic – he stepped into the water and waded down almost its entire length through overhanging shrubbery etc., kampong-like dwellings on the river edge – searching both banks as he went slowly and carefully down its length until, as it approached its mouth, the depth of the water increased and he was forced to abandon his fruitless search for the boy. He had hoped to find the lad perhaps borne by the river flow caught beneath some overhanging branches, or where detritus had dammed the width of the river – but all his efforts were to no avail. He retraced his path – notified the local police of the incident and requested immediate detailed searches of the river onwards from the point of his leaving it.

It was not a clean-smelling river and in his wet, dripping clothes he met the father of the boy and sadly told him of his unsuccessful search – and that a more thorough search was at that moment being made by police using a motor launch. The child's mother, who was several months pregnant, was distraught and it was a sad occasion for Easton, being thanked for his efforts by the tearful mother-to-be.

The father, then about thirty-six years of age, looked at him closely and then said, 'I think we have met before – were you by any chance in Tunisia in early 1943?'

Easton, in an instant knew the reason for the enquiry and replied, 'Yes. You were the MO by the casualty clearing station of Wadi Akarit, I'm sure of it.'

The Major agreed and shook Easton's hand and thanked him for a favour promised long ago and returned in such tragic circumstances. The body of the small boy was found later that day, caught in a wooden-like barrage near the mouth of the river, just inside Singapore Harbour. Accidental death by drowning was the heading of Easton's report, that he wrote so carefully and sorrowfully.

An official commendation for his services was made by the appropriate authorities, and the Major and his wife and newborn child, finished their three-year tour of duty and returned to the UK.

'And you and they never met again, Easton?' asked Holmes – putting down the last page of the story in its proper sequence.

'No, Holmes, that was sixty years ago. Time changes things – people move on in different directions, undertaking different tasks, but the memories never leave one – they just age a little. I shall never forget that family, Holmes, I think I was searching for a child of my own – one that I did not have until many years later. I honestly believe I would have given my own life to save their young boy – I was so determined to find him safe and well, but it was not to be and I went on to become a reasonable investigator – getting close to your exceptional skills – so I'm told. I covered many cases involving so many lost and wasted lives – always trying to find the reasons why such accidents, incidents, occurred – I succeeded sometimes in establishing the link between cause and effect, but had many unsuccessful outcomes, too. Anyway, Holmes, thanks for your help in writing up this incident. What title will you give it?'

'I think "Complementary Gestures" should suffice for the time being, for belated meetings of characters in stories do come about in time.'

'I can't wait Holmes. Thanks again.'

'But this story has a strange ending, Easton – a "ships that pass in the night" sort of thing. You recall your donation of blood you gave over the years, do you not?'

'Yes, had to stop though – age-related nonsense and all that.'

'Well, you remember being phoned several years ago, when you were employed in London – asking if you could help with an urgent blood transfusion case needing your particular blood classification.'

'Yes, indeed, it came from, I think, one of the major hospitals treating children, possibly Great Ormond Street Hospital, it involved a case of crossed mitral valves in a baby's heart. I remember dashing there as quickly as possible, giving the required armful, as I usually told the person in charge, and as I left seeing a group of doctors entering an operation theatre annex, and I wondered if they were involved in the urgent operation in question. But a passing thought.'

'One of those doctors you saw was an honorary consultant surgeon Giles from the Institute of Child Health. He had completed his term of service in the army and had taken up an appointment at Great Ormond Street Hospital. His surgical skills and knowledge were greatly in demand – particularly where children and babies were concerned.'

'And neither of us knew the other was present. How strange, Holmes.'

'Not really, Easton, you good deeders, as I like to call you, don't need to meet – the results of your mutual efforts speak for you – sotto voce of course!'

'Naturally, Holmes, if you say so. Thanks yet again for your own good deed.'

CHAPTER 12

CHARITY BEGINS AT HOME

'I suppose', began Charles Easton to his companion H.C. as they sat together on their favourite bench, in the main garden of HQ Nimbus 9, 'that Holmes does not know that his nurse/carer was the recipient of his donation regarding the surgical operation she underwent all those years ago, or, for that matter, she is aware that he is the person to whom she asked you to convey her heartfelt thanks?'

'Yes, Easton. That is so, but I am aware that the Request was initially filed under her former name, Lamal Khan. Once either of them comes across that entry, Holmes, of all people, will put the facts together and know all there is to know.'

'But of course, H.C., since she is the main archives examiner, a nice term that, I think, she will find the answer in the first place. How do you consider the knowledge might be used?'

'Knowing them both, Easton, it will be a revealing moment to both of them, their unawareness of the bond events made for them long ago, the fact that they became patient and carer, their close working affinity, the obvious trust they have in each other's abilities – all these would, I think, make Holmes believe that coincidences have been stretched a little.'

'Perhaps he is also musing on whether the arrangements

were far from casual arrangements at the time.'

'Well, whatever transpires, Easton, we shall be aware of the fact soon enough.'

'How might that be, H.C.?'

'Shall we just say a close hand-in-hand partnership for them from now on?'

'Would that be literally or physically, do you think?'

'Both, Easton, decidedly both – they were always destined to meet in one world or another, and it is our good fortune they met here in Nimbus 9.'

'None better, H.C. Shall we take our walk and we might encounter the happy pair? – let's loiter near his floral jewels, as he calls them. I see they await his daily inspection and approval.'

'How apt his expression, Easton – a floral jewel, as if one day he would be aware of his own jewellery collection. Do you know their next joint venture relates to a Request I received from a lady who lost both her much loved husband and only son in a road accident. She was close to despair wondering if there was any sense in life any more. The terrible sadness, the grief, and there seemed to be nothing to comfort her in her loss. In order to find once again peace of mind, she was advised to give comfort to a stranger she would meet once she had made a decision to find a solution to her present domestic and emotional problems.'

'And did she follow that advice, H.C.?'

'She did, and Holmes has written a pleasant little story about it. This is his first draft; would you like to read it?'

'With pleasure, H.C. I notice his title is very apt too, "Charity Begins at Home".'

Mrs Rebecca Harding had made her eventual decision to place a small card in the advertisements displayed in the shop window of the village newsagent. She lived alone and had thought long and hard about letting out to rent one of the three bedrooms in her detached house on the edge of the village. Several years ago in a road traffic accident, both her husband and their much beloved son, Anthony, had been killed. She had tried to cope with the terrible sadness of their loss. Stricken with grief she had tried to come to terms with their passing but missed them, their company, their laughter, and most of all their love for her given so freely in so many ways. Small notes and cards written in loving terms last left behind the small objects she had collected over the years – they knew how carefully and tenderly she dusted those ceramics, the small Dresden figurines they had collected on their summer holiday to Germany, the birthplace of her dead husband – or perhaps left behind her few things on her bedside dressing table. Then of course, the many photographs single, double or group poses, the latter taken by an obliging nearby tourist like themselves.

Almost everywhere she looked in the house and garden were memories of father and son. How long she took in her deliberations to donate clothing etc., to the local charity shop and how she could never bear to enter the shop for a long time afterwards in case an item of theirs might still be there on display. All kinds of things to come to terms with, leaving many things as they were, tears shed so easily when finding a letter or notes in books with their unmistakable expansive handwriting with the stressed loops of the Ys and Gs etc. – all indicative, as Anthony would say, of their loving nature expressed especially for her.

So many little finds she made to bring past memories to life, and those findings never seemed to ease the pain and bring lasting comfort. She knew others had gone through that vale of suffering, that she should try to cope to the best of her ability with her grief. She had offered up odd prayers during the day or night for some outside help – but knew always a decision of some kind had to be made by herself as to her altered way of life. And, so, on one of the better springlike days following a bleak, sunless winter, she stood outside the newsagent's shop with the small 'to rent' card in her handbag, deciding eventually to enter the shop.

As she turned, she accidentally bumped into a young man of about twenty-seven years of age who was intent on reading the advertisements on display. The inadvertent collision caused her spectacle case to drop to the ground and the young man instantly picked it up and returned it to her.

She thanked him and his reply was 'A pleasure madam', said with a slight bow of his head.

She then entered the shop, paid a small sum for a week's display of her card reading *furnished bedroom available in detached house, close to all amenities – terms on arrangement. Please phone 0116 945236.*

She had seen similar cards on display mentioning location, size, rental fees quoted, but thought discretion might be more in her line as a beginner. 'Least said soonest mended', as her dead mother used to say.

She walked slowly home, having second thoughts occasionally on her actions, but eventually on reaching home, decided that she had made the correct decision which she was advised to take by someone somewhere unknown.

But a short time later, when cupping in her hands a well-deserved cup of tea for her 'bravery', as she smilingly recollected it to be, the telephone rang. But it was merely an enquiry as to whether loft insulation was required. Since it was already installed by her husband and son the previous year, it was not required thank you. 'Always be courteous just in case', another of her dear mother's remarks. Oh, how she missed her and her comforting arms and words at the time of her loss.

The phone rang again shortly afterwards and a man's voice asked, 'Mrs Harding?'

'Yes,' she replied.

'I saw your ad in the newsagent's window and I wonder if the room is still vacant? If it is still available, might I visit you and have a peep at it, at your convenience entirely of course.'

She liked the voice and thought for a moment she had heard it somewhere before, replied that she was at home now (address details given) and he might see the room at his convenience.

'Might now be of any assistance?' was the reply.

It was, and so within a half-hour or so, the voice as the young man she had met outside the shop earlier arrived, was admitted after a brief scrutiny of recognition and invited to view the room.

It met with his complete approval – as he did to her as a prospective lodger.

Terms were discussed, length of residence agreed, two to three months or so, with perhaps a possibility of extension if he proved an acceptable tenant. Meals were no problem as his needs were modest in that connection, but he added; the odd cup of tea would not go amiss and might, if supplied, be added to the monthly or weekly rent.

She found herself taking to this polite, cheerful young man, and heard herself very boldly say, 'Would you like a cup of tea as I am in my own tea-drinking mood at present.'

'I'd like nothing more, Mrs Harding.'

'Am I to call you Anthony or Mr Peterson?'

'Anthony would be fine.'

They sat in the sun-filled sitting room, eyes on each other, tea in hand and a small plate of biscuits within easy reach, and talked. She made brief mention that she was the owner of the house and its only occupant, and learnt that he was a former member of HM forces, had recently completed his term of service, and had been born in Flensburg, Germany some twenty-seven years ago. His parents, a German father and a Scottish mother, were divorced and he was their only child. He arranged to collect his small items of luggage at the railway station, and would move into his new domain within an hour or so.

And this duly took place, but only after his enquiry as to whether he might wipe up the used crockery before he left. Such duties were gracefully declined, and he took his leave with the duplicate house key in his possession. She had made no mention of furniture and fittings deposit as she had been advised by a neighbour who also had a lodger. He had simply paid the month's rent in advance and made no quibbling remarks as to amount charged, which in all truth was half the sum her neighbour charged her tenant.

But that was unimportant. In his absence, she quickly dusted his room (as she mentally now called it), put out towels etc., in the en suite toilet facilities. A fresh towel, bar of soap, and the usual 'roll of bumph', as he later called it.

She had taken an instant liking to him – his cheerful disposition, his kindness and blatant honesty (she was a good assessor of such traits, she knew instinctively), made her think how fortunate was her decision to alter her way of life, and to have such a nice first lodger – for she knew, or so she thought, there would be others in due course.

But how wrong she was on this latter assumption.

He remained in her house for several years, filled all the gaps in her life, got the unused Ford car out of the garage, tuned up its engine, charged up its battery, put new tyres on, had it MOT'd and, since she could not drive (vision not up to the necessary standard), drove her to friends, relatives of her dead husband, and one summer, drove her to Germany. Even the return boat trip by ferry from Hamburg to Harwich was a sheer delight. He spoke a good German, got along well with all those met and shared laughter became once more the order of the day.

When Anthony eventually married a wonderful German

girl from Cologne, she was maid of honour, acting mother by proxy and her tears no longer of sorrow were of joy on that occasion, and many times thereafter.

Anthony and his wife and small daughter Rebecca, after her own name, lived quite close by.

'And, Connie Lamal, your turn to supply the happy ending to this tale.'

'Let it stand as it is, Derrick, we have our own. Let that suffice – and thank you for writing both stories, theirs and ours. Oh, Holmesy, will we ever get to the end of these Celestial Requests?'

'We already have, young Lamal, we already have.'

'Yes, you are right, let it just be a final sentence.'

'And that being?'

'And once I knew grief and sorrow but now I know faith, hope, love and charity stay with us forever. But the greatest of these is charity.'

'Don't forget love as well, Lamal.'

'I never do, Derrick Holmes, I never do. Like charity, it is said to be the sweetest sometimes when love is silent – like your loving gift to me long, long ago.'

CHAPTER 13

PRIMA VERA AND OTHER MUSINGS

'A distant branch of my family, many, many years ago, settled in some verdant valley and called this celestial spring of ours today – Prima Vera – a very apt term for the first green of spring, don't you think so, Easton?'

'I do indeed, H.C. That was in those Mundo years, of course?'

'Yes, and even in this day and age, those bright intellects down there on the Speck of Dust, wonder if there is even one blade of grass, one leaf, exactly like another and, there isn't – they are all different, in weight, size, format.'

'It's understandable, H.C., for the true size of the universe is not known to them – I believe they call it "unlimited space".'

'I wonder also, Easton, if they know that there are more galaxies, stars, planets, etc., in that universal space than in all the grains of sand on their beaches?'

'A somewhat stiff order, H.C. – the mysteries of the heavens are their main thought and some surprising results have been obtained from their telescopic observations.'

'Such a pity, Easton, that aggressive warring tendencies still abound in many areas and locations.'

'Sadly, that is so, H.C. If only they had a few live Conan Derrick Holmeses to show them the errors of their ridiculous wasteful ways.'

'About our Holmes, Easton, he is "having a go", as he calls it, at poetry at present. He has by him two books of verse by his friend and former comrade, Vernon Scannell and is busily following Vernon's guidance in avoiding ravid doggerel of the performance poets and elegant gibberish. Now there's a statement of intent for you!'

'I remember Vernon once writing to me years ago that he subscribed to the remarks of Paul Vallery, "that a man is a poet if the difficulties inherent in his art are providing him with ideas; he is not a poet if they deprive him of ideas".'

'One thing that shines out in his poems is his great belief in its human forms – and, it should touch the heart.'

'I agree wholeheartedly with that, H.C., the Speck of Dust folk have still yet to grapple correctly with that four-letter word – but, they will one day, no doubt. I have always liked the introduction of the love element in that reference to you as in that "Old Man River" poignant song, sung in the Deep South of the United States. The chapel songs and hymns sung with such fervour, longing, even sadness of belonging elsewhere in time long ago.'

'It still goes on, Easton, thankfully. But I just don't say nothing as I roll towards the tidal waters of the sea – for in my ripples, waves, stirrings, I sing with them – knowing that it is the ebb tide that takes them towards us at Nimbus 9 and the flood tide that brings them to us.'

'And, H.C., what musical joy they bring to so many of us non-cotton or -potato planters.'

'A great country, that United States of America – great in many ways yet to unfold. Strange, Easton, how our talks always seem to circle around our Holmes and his accomplishments.'

'A pleasant subject on which to say goodnight, H.C.'

'Yes, goodnight, Easton – ditto tomorrow?'

'Ditto it is, H.C.'

'Oh, by the way, Easton, have you noticed that vast

generous country the USA has a City of Angels?'

'Yes, Los Angeles and its Palo Alto region have quite a few small angels resident there. There is even an avenue named the Point of Love – I suppose a point of direction to their whereabouts?'

'Who knows, Easton? Who knows, save us? Goodnight yet again.'

'Goodnight, H.C. Bless you.'

'Borrowing my line again?'

'This week's deliberate error, H.C.! – the critics are sure to find it!'

CELESTIAL REQUESTS

'I was about to say, H.C., that it is strange, but of course, it is not so, that almost every Celestial Request received relates to a person or persons other than the one making the Request. It is not a question of self-orientation, but rather a plea on behalf of others.'

'A selfless, unselfish Request, you mean, Easton?'

'Yes, indeed. I suppose the same relates to the other Nimbuses in your domain?'

'Well, at Triquinnal Assembly Meetings I attend, each Chief Celeste has remarked on this fact – suggesting all our mutual improvement concepts are working on the right lines. There are many issues in the universe needing our attention. Causal creation is still being developed in some parts as you know, but I am confident that our particular Speck of Dust holds some wonderful human material.'

'Yes, H.C. I know Holmes agrees with you on that point. I heard him humming (well he calls it singing) "Just a Song at Twilight" once. He is a sentimental soul where that Speck of Dust is concerned. He believes that once the full, true strength of love is truly realised there – our work on Guardian Angel concept is done. They will realise that each of them holds within themselves their own Guardian Angel. Many have an inkling of it now – those who put their lives on the line for others, motivated no doubt by that Greater Love.'

EPILOGUE

It had been a pleasant evening of 'Celestial Conviviality', as Easton named it, with H.C. and his companions at HQ Nimbus 9. The matter of Holmes returning to his role as Chief Investigating Officer had been settled, and Easton had accepted most willingly the vacant position of Chief Secretary to H.C.

Those present at the meeting had been ministers of all the many other HQ Nimbus 9 branches, Historical Branch, Archives, Transportation, Administration, Accommodation – an almost bewildering number of offices, all staffed, Easton thought, by first-class people. Competence, loyalty, intelligence – all so obvious traits – but one special trait linked them. They had been personally and individually chosen by H.C. himself.

When discussing this observation he had made re these ministerial grades with H.C. he learnt that each minister chosen had, at one time or another, read the writing of an eminent philosopher, Bertram Russell, given the title *The Conquest of Happiness*.

Easton had not read the work in question but that evening resolved to do so. Select Bibliographic and Sources Branch provided him with a copy of an opening chapter of a book *Just Passing On* written by the Chief Secretary C.S. of Pre-Assignment and Enquiries Branch. Its contents he read as follows:

A man of adequate stability and zest will surmount all misfortunes by the emergence after each blow of an interest in life and the world which cannot be narrowed down so much as to make one fatal. To be defeated by one loss or even by several is not something to be admired as sensibility, but something to be deplored as a failure in vitality. All one's affections are at the mercy of death which may strike down those whom we love, at any moment. It is therefore necessary that our lives should not have that narrow intensity, which puts the whole meaning and purpose on life at the mercy of an accident.

One should harken to his words, they contain a degree of comforting courage. When I first read these words, I thought our old army expression (particularly when in doubt of precise details of an objective) 'bash on regardless' summed up our attitude to military adventures and misadventures. I certainly think this reflects my attitude to life's fortunes and misfortunes – save that in bashing on regardless – one always took pains to regard those not as fortunate as oneself. This I have, on many occasions, tried to do, but not always with success. As a small observational aside, I do not know whether Bertram Russell ever had occasion to go for a soldier or as a member of the other armed services, but had he been employed in the former capacity, in aggressive and warlike circumstances, whether he might have entertained such a beautiful vision of that unseen and tantalising Hereinafter. But a personal viewpoint – perhaps he resides there as I write – who knows? After all, a well-known intellectual Prof. Dawkins believes (and rightly so?) that there were many duplicate multi-universes out there in the vastness of space – perhaps, Bertram Russell's Hereinafter is but one of them? Again who knows? But, as Charles Dickens says, one must not meander, and the foregoing does indicate such meandering should be curbed if there is a story to be told – one should harken to such words from a wonderful writer as Charles Dickens.

Easton thought the gist of the article was to the effect that whatever difficulties assailed mankind, these should be accepted as part of the experience of life itself. They were to be faced up to, overcome if possible, and there was to be no need to rely on outside help from a tantalising place he (Russell) referred to as a beautiful Hereinafter.

Each of H.C.'s chosen band of ministers had coped bravely with many difficulties in their lives – such as vicarious physical and mental injuries, family grief and loss, domestic disappointments of some magnitude and yet, in each case, had battled on against many odds, brought up decent families and helped others in many ways. They made the usual human mistakes, tried to right their individual wrongs, and, in the main, had led decent, honest lives.

'Battlers All' H.C. called them. Once referred to in that Speck of Dust as "the salt of the earth". Not one of them came from the ranks of Ruritania, as Holmes called the sprigs of blood of a different hue. They were simply good, honest men and women, tried severely in the heat of worldly fortunes and misfortunes, and yet came good, as one of the Australians among their number phrased it. They had, between them, amassed a considerable amount of knowledge, intelligence and wisdom but above all, a love of their fellow men, women and children.

Holmes once said, 'I'd like to grow like them one day' (possibly, in his modesty, unaware of the fact that he is already one of their number).

It has proved to be a pleasant task, to record these instances of Celestial Requests, and their outcomes all from a fanciful imagination of sorts, of course. But there might be a Nimbus 9 where a Highest Celeste is invariably attended by those faithful select until the end of time itself? Again, who knows if Bertram Russell himself is not one of those faithful ones who have pursued happiness and found it needs not to be conquered to attain it – it is free to all.